L'académie

By

R. C. WALDUN

LITERARY. Publication
an imprint of
www.rcwaldun.com

First paperback edition September 2021

ISBN 978-0-6489632-0-2 (paperback)
ISBN 978-0-6489632-1-9 (ebook)

To Ila-Rose, My Muse

"Innocence, Once Lost, Can Never Be Regained.
Darkness, Once Gazed Upon, Can Never Be Lost."
— John Milton

CONTENTS

Chapter 1

The indicator turned green as Eddington crossed the road in a straight line. A gentle wind blew through The Regime, and there weren't many people out. Pieces of rubbish whirled along the ground, but someone would pick them up eventually. Eddington touched his ears and made sure the buds were still in place; they weren't working as well as they used to. Along the street, other people passed by him, all walking in the same straight line, all wearing the same earpieces, the same blank expression.

Eddington was wearing a gray blazer issued by The Regime. It didn't keep him warm against the emerging cold weather, but if he walked a little faster, he felt fine. At a road junction, he saw a coffee cup rolling in a circle. He wanted to pick it up, to clear some of the trash cluttering the street, but all that mattered was getting a warm drink. A few more turns, and Eddington saw the café. Along the way, he passed roamers crowding the streets, all wearing the exact same style of blazer in different colors. One in navy, walking ahead. Another in white, peeking out of the bakery. Once in a while, tall, militant figures in black suits lurked in the shadows, their backs erect and faces blank.

He stopped in front of the café and took a deep breath, one he could see in the crisp afternoon air. He looked through the large landing window, fogged along the edges. Past his own reflection, he saw his friends from L'Académie, lying leisurely across the café's couches, having a casual chat. Through the window, all he saw were the motions of their gestures and the rocking of their heads. He opened the door, and the muffled voices became clear.

"Are you sure that was an Ester Group?" said a man neatly dressed in a navy blazer.

"Now, no! And there, there is where you and I differ."

"Cut me some slack; I'm from the History branch." He took a slow sip from his cup.

"Chemical Engineering." The man sat back, crossing his arms.

"Not a Humanitarian, are you?"

"Humanitarians? What, you're going to work at The Plant after you're done?"

"Right, right, right." In the midst of the exchange, the gray blazer noticed Eddington from the corner of his eye. "You! Eddington? Ha, right back at it. Gentlemen, he just came back from L'Académie!" He stood up and patted Eddington's shoulder. Eddington remembered how he was always so talkative.

"How was it?" the gray blazer asked.

He didn't know. He was in the coffee shop, and he knew information he hadn't known before, and he hadn't wandered from his path once on the walk over, and he—

Eddington started at the second tap on his shoulder. "Just… all the normal things."

"Come on. Tell us about it." The gray blazer sat back down. Eddington looked down at his own clothing, then back up at the man. They were both from the History branch. "Now you know what I really wish, Ed? I wish they'd given you that part already."

"Which part?"

"The evolution of French political philosophy." The words came out of his mouth without effort. He was the Man of History.

"I'm not sure." Eddington shrugged.

"Well, only one way to find out." The Man of History drained his cup. "Tell me a little something about Voltaire."

"*Letters Concerning the English Nation*, which advocated various forms of religious freedom. As he stated, 'If one religion only were allowed in England—'" He stopped. He hadn't known that the previous day.

"Well, well. They did drill it into you." The Man of History clapped as he made his way to the counter. Eddington stood silent.

"You, there. Hey, put that thing away." The Man of History was at the counter, speaking to someone in a beige blazer. "Playing smart, aren't you? You know if they find out, they'll…" He paused as the beige blazer brought a pipe to his mouth. "Wait, aren't you a Linguist?"

"Right." The beige blazer took the pipe out of his mouth. "Are you looking for something?"

The Man of History cleared his throat. "I happen to know a little something about… aspects of semantic patterning, let's say."

The Linguist made a funny sniffling noise. "There are many aspects. And I'm not even sure if semantic patterning is a good enough term to cover it. Hmm. Personification, oxymoron, pun, simile, lexicon…"

Eddington still lingered at the door, wondering at the words rolling out of the Linguist's mouth. All those theories he'd never explore, the knowledge he'd never acquire. He only had dates and facts. That's all a Historian was.

"Wow. Hat's off to you," said the Man of History. He turned toward Eddington with a smirk. "Oh, Ed, how I love this." His eyebrows furrowed, noticing Eddington hovering by the door. "Are you all right?"

"Yeah, yeah, just..." Eddington shifted his feet to and fro. All eyes were on him. In a fit of panic, Eddington needed to get out of the café. His heart beat frantically against his rib cage, and he felt frozen in fear, rendering him unable to speak or breathe. "You all keep talking. Don't... don't mind me."

"What's wrong?" The Man of History walked up to Eddington. "I see. Hero of two worlds? Amongst Society of Thirty throughout the Revolution?"

"I... Marquis de... The Duke... La... La Rochefoucauld?" He needed to get out of the café.

"No. *La Rochefoucauld* wasn't him."

Everything became a blur to Eddington.

The Man of History continued. "Are you sure you're—"

"I'm good! I'm fine." Eddington pushed the Man of History away.

"Whoa! Calm your—"

Outside, a gush of strong wind whirled, and a muffled whistle made its way through the café's glass. Eddington whipped his head up, brought to life by the sound.

"I need to go back."

"Go back to what?" the Man of History asked.

"My Complex."

"Oh, right. Your Complex is near The Wall, yeah? Just a few streets down?" The Man of History looked out of the fogged window. Eddington could see the humming bud in his left ear.

"Yes, it is." Eddington calmed a little.

The Man of History sat back down. "Off you go. Tomorrow, then?"

Eddington was already out the café's door.

He walked in a straight line, guided by movements of habit. His own feet were not in his control as the earbuds hummed in his ears. He'd never known what the buds were for, but everyone else wore them, so he knew they were essential. After a few turns amongst the windy streets, he saw The Wall. It towered over him, bearing down on his stooped stature. Some told him The Wall was a district marker, a check mark that separated huge groups of people. Like the earbuds, it was an important part of his life. Along the base of The Wall, a line of guards in masks carried machine guns; they stood straight-backed as those masks rendered them expressionless. After a few more seconds of looking at The Wall, Eddington turned away and walked up the stairs to his room in The Complex.

The lighting system flicked on as he entered his room, and the triple glass-paneled screen came to life. A speaker from the ceiling aired: "Afternoon, Eddington. What would you like to watch tonight?"

"Please, just the usual today."

"No problem. Please wait."

"Thank you." Eddington settled himself on the couch as he took off his blazer. In front of him, a show loaded, and the lights dimmed. Eddington spiraled into the motions, the actions and periodic thrills of the content of the triple screens. As the show progressed, something distended within Eddington. He had felt it a little earlier at the café: a hollow void in his gut slowly expanding and warping within him. The more he flowed through the motions of L'Académie and roamed the streets, the larger the void grew. The more he tried to immerse himself in the images on the screen, the hollower he felt.

The muffled sounds of Eddington's triple screen's speakers traveled out of his shutters, joining the muffled sounds coming from other rooms. Together, all formed a cacophony of tangled noises as different shows loaded on different screens. Black suits still stalked the streets. Another gush of wind traced its way along the buildings while a man in a long dark coat stopped to listen to the buzz coming from The Complex. He chuckled and shook his head as he turned into an alleyway.

***

Eddington opened his eyes. The glow of the early sunrise brightened the shutters' gaps, casting strings of white light on the bedsheets. He felt recharged and ready to take on the day, but he couldn't stop fixating on one thing: throughout the night, the content of L'Académie kept creeping into his muddled brain. Fragments of thoughts, some about Abbé Sieyès, some about the Tennis Court Oath, crowded his mind. They rendered his fragile sleep a series of periodic dips in and out of lapses of mental imageries and words. Some were fragments of dreams, others dry facts.

Eddington rubbed his eyes as he got out of bed. The piercing sunlight was the only life in the room. Everything else was gray: his shirt, his bedsheets, his nightstand. Dragging his feet on the carpeted floor, Eddington made his way into the living room.

The speaker aired: "Good morning, sir. How are you today?"

"Not bad." He stretched after the night's sleep. "What time is it now?"

"Your session will begin in two hours. Please get ready if you wish. By the way, those buds, have you been wearing them?"

"Yes, of course, of course. Last night…"

"Yes, sir?"

"I was getting these weird in and out… It's hard to…"

"No worries, sir, it's quite common. The Cross happened to you. Maybe you should get the buds checked out at The Corner?"

"Good idea."

"Appointment booked. It is in thirty minutes."

"Thank you." He looked around his room. "The Duke de La Rochefoucauld… No, can't be. What is it? Maybe he was right—I'm not up to that part yet."

"Sir?"

"Sorry, I was—"

"It's okay, sir. La Rochefoucauld: one of the most prominent families of the French aristocracy. One of its early members in the seventeenth century was the author of a book of aphorisms that shaped French culture."

"Yes, right." He knew those details perfectly well, but the fact that he couldn't yet access the name of that man, the "hero of two worlds" who belonged to the Society of Thirty, distressed him a little. He walked toward the wardrobe and took out his blazer and pants issued by The Regime. Different branches of students wore different colored blazers. History wore gray. Linguists wore beige. Chemical Engineers wore navy. The Prefects were the only ones who wore black suits. Eddington tucked in his shirt and tightened his belt. After securing the buds in his ears, he threw the blazer over his shoulders.

Out he went to the street. It was not a windy day. The morning sun hung like an egg, the white edges extending out to merge with the cloudy sky. "The Corner. Appointment in twenty minutes," he murmured. "The Cross? The Cross." His hands were in his pockets as he walked with his head down.

"Sir?" called a deep voice. Eddington halted his steps and turned. To his shock, it was a Prefect. "No talking out loud in the streets." The Prefect tilted his head; Eddington leaned back.

"Your buds are not working well."

"I'm heading to The Corner now."

"Right," the Prefect uttered in his formal voice. "Be careful next time."

"Well, thank you." Eddington tensed up.

The Prefect took a step away from him. "Good day, sir," he said as he wandered off with his blanked face and militant poise. Eddington never quite liked the Prefects.

A few streets over, Eddington arrived at The Corner. The building blended in with everything else in the district: stark gray and functional, meant to serve a purpose. The only thing that separated it from the rest of the block was a sliding glass entrance door. Eddington walked through, going up to the screen to sign in.

The screen's camera recognized Eddington and turned the speakers on. "Sir, your appointment is in ten minutes. Please, take a seat."

"Thank you." Eddington glanced around. Rows of stark white seats stared back at him, with the occasional person slouching down as they fiddled in wait.

"When is your next session at L'Académie, sir?"

Eddington cleared his throat. "Ninety minutes."

"Your branch, sir?"

"History."

"Oh, I see. Humanitarians, well—they require constant maintenance. Otherwise, The Cross will happen."

"It happened last night." He rubbed his palms together.

"Your family, are they all from the History branch?"

"Yes. Mother... Mother was from the English branch. She works at the entries of The Plant now, you know, maintaining L'Académie? Father, well..."

"Yes, sir?"

"Never saw him again after his arrest." A deep breath in and out.

"Yes, sir."

"One day, he just went mad. Spouting those—those words. I couldn't understand them at all. Crazy. That's why after last night, I was..."

"Yes, sir?"

"It was—weird. The Cross. Why? Why does it happen?"

"Sir—"

"Did The Cross get my father arrested?"

The screen's indicator turned from green to red. "Your earbuds are indeed malfunctioning. Take a seat, sir."

"Please get them fixed." Eddington paced around the registration desk.

"Your appointment is in ten minutes."

"Yes, I know that."

"Please, take a seat."

There it was: a man begging a machine to fix him. But Eddington knew he couldn't be fixed; no one knew what The Cross was. The only thing Eddington knew was the buds would keep The Cross from happening.

Across the street, the man in the long dark coat stood, watching Eddington through the glass. He chuckled again and rejoined the passing students, all in blazers.

Chapter 2

"Seventy minutes… seventy minutes."

Eddington wandered out of The Corner, disoriented after the consult meant to fix his earbuds. His pace quickened; he wanted to catch the transport at the station in time for his session at L'Académie. As he walked, Eddington couldn't help but trace his eyes across the electronic screens hanging on the walls of the gray buildings. Black text against white backgrounds proclaimed the tenants of The Regime alongside transport route information:

- *L'Académie.*

- *Remember to report signs of Double-Rods.*

- *Knowledge is Power.*

- *District-E, Station B, Bay Seven, Express to L'Académie.*

- *Report Double-Rods to Prefects.*

The messages reminded Eddington of his part in The Regime. He was a cog, aware of its place in the system, aware that all he had to do was follow the rules, and everything would continue chugging along.

District-E, where he lived, was dedicated to educating a special class of citizens. His mother once lived in District-E, but now she worked for The Plant, a data-management facility in a neighboring district. Despite their different roles, each district featured the screens dominating the streets. No one could forget knowledge was power, nor could they forget the danger of the Double-Rods. Eddington never minded the screens, but he did mind the Prefects.

Reminder to all citizens of District-E: Report any Double-Rods found.

He kept marching toward the station, avoiding the Prefects' eyes as he passed them.

Please report any signs of Double-Rods.

A Physicist once told Eddington, "In a physical experiment, Double-Rods tend to conform to a non-uniform range of motions."

"But what does that have to do with The Regime?"

"Well, they introduce patterns of chaos."

"What does that mean?"

"Maybe Double-Rods will mess with our knowledge?" The man in the brown blazer scratched his head. "I've never actually seen Double-Rods myself. At least not around here."

"Right… Double-Rods." His steps took him to the station, where The Boxes skated to a stop in large bays, waiting for the next pack of passengers. Each Box brought District-E citizens to their desired place, going in an endless loop of there and back and there and back. As Eddington approached the station, he saw a crowd of people gathered at Bay Seven, the express line to L'Académie.

He disappeared into the crowd, another person wearing another blazer waiting to flow into The Box at Bay Seven. Just as he was stepping into the windowless carriage, Eddington caught a glimpse of someone standing across the station. He wasn't wearing a blazer; instead, a long coat drifted behind him.

The Box started to move, and the man in the long coat stuffed his hands into his pockets. His eyes were imbued with a contemplative look; his face wrinkled with markers of age. He watched The Box getting farther away from the station—Eddington was on his way toward L'Académie. The man sighed. "That fool." A Prefect showed up behind the man in the long coat.

"Sir, no speaking out on the streets." Again, with the Prefects' sternness.

"Yes, yes. Sorry," the man in the long coat said.

"This is your final warning, sir."

"Thank you." He took his hands from his pockets and rubbed them together.

The erect figure walked off. The man in the long coat shook his head. *Utter bores.* He rolled the words over in his head, wanting to avoid the Prefect's attention. "Right, right, right." He tucked his neck into the popped collar of his winter coat and wandered down the street away from the station.

People can't even feel the cold now. At least, not here.

***

The seats were steel-framed with beige cushions, similar to the ones at The Corner. There wasn't very much variation in The Regime. Despite the fact that each carriage could hold sixty-five people, the seats were never full. No one wanted to sit next to someone for an entire ride, afraid of being close to a stranger for that long. In the off-chance they did, talking on The Box was prohibited, and there was no reason to talk anyway. All of the passengers stayed in their own little worlds. All looked down, not around. All had those humming earbuds and glowing screens.

Like everyone else, Eddington lost himself in the moving pixels of the issued screen. He always got lost in the images fluttering in front of his eyes; it hastened the time spent on The Box, making the senseless monotony of the windowless ride a bit more bearable. But that day, something was different. The hollow void from the previous night was back, burrowing in him, eating away at everything he knew was right. He tried to immerse himself into the screen. He tried to quiet his thoughts. "The Duke de… The Marquis de…" He fidgeted as the right hand that held the screen began to tremble, and he wondered if they actually fixed his buds at The Corner. His breaths became shallower. In his chest, a sensation he could not describe ballooned. The Prefect at the back stood up.

"Sir." The Prefect walked toward Eddington. "Are you well?"

"I…" Eddington's right hand continued to tremor. Something was wrong, he knew, but he didn't have the words to explain exactly what that "something" was.

"Everything's fine?" The Prefect tilted his head to look at Eddington's ears. "Your buds are working well?"

"Well, I…" Eddington locked his screen with his trembling hand.

"Yes, sir?"

"Don't worry about it." Eddington forced the tremor to stop as he slipped the screen into his right pocket.

"Anything you need, sir. I'll be back there."

"Thank you."

The Prefect went back to his seat. Eddington looked around The Box, wondering if anyone took notice of his run-in with The Prefect. But every man and woman, all wearing the same style of blazer, had their eyes glued to the screens in front of them. The tremor of his right hand calmed, but the sensation he couldn't quite describe swelled. Eddington unliked those Prefects. There it was again: that word, *unlike*. That was the best he could do to describe it. "Unlike," he uttered. The word seemed to give him a strange kind of relief. *Unlike. I unlike The Box—The Prefects.* He didn't have the courage to say those words aloud, but he did mull them over in his head. The tremor in his right hand crept back.

Rousseau, Locke, Voltaire, The Spirit of Laws by Montesquieu, government. Our government, The Regime, L'Académie…

The Prefect at the back narrowed his eyes.

The Cross—The Cross happened again. Damn it.

"Is everything all right, sir? Sir?" The Prefect came to Eddington again.

"Fine… ah, fine. You… I had—"

The Prefect knelt down beside Eddington's seat. Some passengers on The Box lifted their head; a word or two spoken by a Prefect on The Box was not unusual, but an entire conversation, let alone two of them, was unheard of. Eddington took a deep breath. "When… will The Box… get there?"

He needed air. He needed to get out of The Box. He couldn't stand it any longer. The Prefect pointed at the screen displaying the stops. The speaker aired: "Citizens, the next stop will be The Central Square of L'Académie."

Upon hearing the announcement, the other passengers stood up all at once, heads still down, eyes still glued to the screens. The spectacle swelled the unease in Eddington even more.

I need to get out—now! I need to get out!

The doors slid open, and the passengers streamed out all at once. They moved in tandem, seeming to be one big organism. Finally, Eddington was at the door. Out he went as he took a deep, long breath.

A citizen of District-E, I go to L'Académie, and I need the knowledge to get a good job beyond The Wall—

"Sir?" The Prefect also got off The Box. Eddington was still trying to catch his breath.

"I'm sorry?" Eddington looked up at the Prefect.

"Do you require assistance, sir?"

"It's quite fine. Sorry. It's… I'm fine now. My appointment is in half an hour. I have to go."

"Goodbye, sir." The Prefect walked off.

He unliked that place. He unliked everything there was.

He walked over to the Square and arrived at L'Académie. It didn't look like much: a single-story gray building, blending in with every other place in The Regime. But L'Académie was deceptive; most of it was an underground facility. Apparently, learning was optimized if there were no distractions, and that included windows to the outside world.

Varied entrances separated people into their fields. Before, there was a mix of all colors. In the square of L'Académie, neatly organized files of colored blazers shuffled along. Prefects monitored their every move.

Eddington merged into the line of gray blazers at the entrance of the History branch. As he walked amongst the file, his unease calmed. He no longer "unliked"; he was no longer struggling for air. He felt quite relieved and was ready to learn something new. Maybe he'd go talk to the Man of History after his session.

***

The session at L'Académie was like any other day. At a checkpoint, they were separated and assigned cubicles where each had a glass-paneled screen and headgear on a swinging metal arm. After hearing some brief instructions, all went through a brief setup on the screens and placed the headgear on their heads. Typical sessions lasted for three hours. After that, they were dismissed to The Square.

Along the paths of the darkening streets whirled the late afternoon breeze. Eddington felt a slight chill as he walked and wanted a warm drink. Everything would be fine. He'd go back to the café and talk to the Man of History. Eddington had his hands in his pockets and tucked his neck in a little, and after a few turns along the footpath, he arrived at the café.

Eddington saw the Man of History through the fogged window. He opened the door as the man stood up.

"Hello." Eddington entered.

"Did you get that part down? Finally?" The Man of History reached for his coffee cup.

"It was the Marquis de Lafayette. Society of Thirty, nobleman, hero of the American Revolution."

"Great. You see? Finally."

"And I also found out the Duke de La Rochefoucauld was a seventeenth-century nobleman who authored a series of maxims and aphorisms."

"Very good. Very good." The Man of History straightened his gray blazer's lapels as he sipped out of his cup. "You are learning."

"Yeah." The café was quite empty. The Man of History's friends weren't around, but Eddington still refused to sit across from him. His right hand started tremoring again.

"What's wrong?"

"It's nothing." Eddington shoved his hand into his pocket.

"Okay, well. Let's see if they gave you the good parts. Tennis Court?"

"The Tennis Court Oath, twentieth of June. Members of the Third Estate were locked out of Estates General. They moved to a tennis court and facilitated the formation of the National Assembly through taking a collective oath." The words flowed out of him without effort.

"Very good." The Man of History smiled and sipped again. "In no time, my friend, you'll be at my level."

"Yeah." Eddington forced a smile. The Man of History looked out the fogged window.

Double-Rod, The Cross, Tennis Court…

The hand in his right pocket tremored more violently than before. A moment later, his entire right arm began to shake.

"I, uh… sorry, I have to go." Eddington paced around the café's floor.

"Go where?"

"The Complex."

"What in the world is happening to you?"

"I… I don't know."

"Well, tomorrow then?"

"May—maybe."

He rushed out of the café as he breathed in a lungful of cold afternoon air.

I am Eddington. I was… sent here… to District-E, to be educated at L'Académie… Lafayette, Voltaire, biens nationaux, National Assembly…

Those thoughts were not his own. They sprang out of him. They messed with his world. His hands started tremoring again; his breathing shallowed. He stared at the night sky but wasn't sure what he was looking for. Soon, his racing thoughts came to a sudden halt as a hand landed on his shoulder.

"Sir, are you all right?" It was a Prefect again.

"Fine." He shoved the shaking hand deeper into his pocket, hoping the folds of fabric would hide the tremors.

"Please get back to your Complex, sir."

"Yes, yes. On my way." Eddington walked away from the Prefect.

The indescribable sensation careened within him. His palms were wet. His face contorted. "I really, really—unlike—unlike the Prefects." The word seemed to have lost its ability to comfort him, but there was no other way to express his state.

District-E. L'Académie, a screen on his right displayed.

He walked faster and looked down, avoiding the screens.

Please report any Double-Rods.

"No! Shut up," he murmured. He walked fast, looking down. His only company were the screens looming over him.

Please report to L'Académie at your designated sessions.

"Screens... *Cahiers*... Louis the sixteenth..."

Knowledge is power.

"I... I..."

"Hate." A voice—a word. It didn't come from the screens.

Eddington lifted his head. Whoever said the word had already passed him. He turned around and saw a man in a long coat walking away from him.

Hate.

He dared not sound it out. The word had such a charge, such a buzz.

I hate those Prefects; I hate The Box.

He stopped as he reached the street leading up to The Wall. From where he stood, he saw the streetlights aligned, illuminating a swath of ground in front of The Wall. Militant guardsmen still stood in a straight file, equipped with machine guns. Whatever was beyond The Wall must have been good—the screens told everyone of those wonders beyond. And the way to go beyond The Wall was to submit to L'Académie. One more year, and he'd be out—Eddington was nearing the end of his four-year program. The tremors settled as Eddington let out a breath. He took a left turn and went up to his Complex.

"Afternoon. Tiring day at L'Académie, sir? You look quite exhausted."

The lighting system kicked into gear.

"It's nothing. I walked too fast."

"Your meal, sir?"

"Didn't have time for lunch."

"Double portion today?"

"Single portion, please."

"Program, sir?"

"The same one as yesterday. Thank you."

Eddington stretched out on the couch after tossing his blazer on the floor. The three glass panels drew him in. All the sensations from earlier—the sweaty palms, The Box, the tremoring hand, the word "hate"—dissolved at the sight of the drama on the screen. Nothing but the panels seemed relevant. His earbuds hummed, working wonders within.

Chapter 3

For one day of the week, sessions at L'Académie were suspended. The Regime had strict policies about that. A student could only take a maximum of six sessions per week. Or else, as described in the official rules, there might be neurological risks.

Eddington was lying on his bed in the morning, staring at the white ceiling. He didn't remember how much time he'd spent watching the triple screen the night before, nor did he remember exactly when he went to bed. Sounds of people conversing seeped through the white wall of Eddington's bedroom; maybe the man next door forgot to turn off his triple screen the previous night. He wished a night's sleep would be enough to drown out all the chaos, that it was a dream or a scene from the screens. But with mental clarity in the morning and an entire day left to himself, his mind wandered back to the same state as the day before.

"I was on The Box. I felt ungood. Prefects... I..." He paused as he stepped down from the bed and looked into the living room: the home system was still on, monitoring his moves. He'd heard stories of people who vanished suddenly after speaking a forbidden word. The indicator on the main console turned red, and Prefects would come beat the door down. One day, the person was there, and the next, they were gone. All because of one careless word. But Eddington didn't know what he couldn't say—the list of prohibited words wasn't published—so he always took the safest route. He said nothing.

I hate those Prefects.

He could do nothing more than turn those words in his head. At least Prefects couldn't break into his mind. The word brought Eddington back to the other day, where he'd first heard it. Who was that man who'd given it to him? Why was he in a long coat instead of a blazer? He made his way into the living room.

The indicator turned blue as the speaker aired: "Sir, are you well this morning?"

"I'm all right." Still, that sensation burrowed in his chest. Every one of his private moves was monitored.

"Anything to do today, sir?"

"Café." The majority of his interactions were with machines. Most of the time, the speaker in his room gave him companionship. But that day, he felt even more alone. He made his way to the washroom, hoping a shower would reset his mind and help everything make sense again. But it didn't. He got out and dressed in the neat gray uniform and adjusted the earbuds in his ears. A brief glimpse in the mirror; he was who he was on any other day.

***

Eddington was back out on the streets. The sun peeked out of the clouds periodically, and the streets darkened and brightened. An electric box made those *tick, tock, tick, tock* noises as he passed it. He worried one day that thing might explode. He headed for the café; perhaps the Man of History would be there for a chat. On his way, he saw the screens again:

L'Académie, center of learning.

Attention citizens of District-E: report any signs of Double-Rods.

He passed them with his eyes down, not wanting a repeat of the day before—he knew attracting too much of the Prefects' attention would end badly. His father showed him that. After crossing a few streets, he was at the café and saw the Man of History sitting at his usual spot, sipping a cup of coffee. He entered the café; the Man of History looked up.

"Hey! Ed!"

"Hey." He walked up to the counter to order.

"What was with you yesterday? And the day before?"

"I was tired."

"Uh-huh." The Man of History set down his cup.

A short stretch of silence.

"You want a drink?"

"Already on it." Eddington tapped the counter.

A screen provided him with a range of options. He clicked hot chocolate, and the machine set to work, brewing his drink. All Eddington had to do was collect it at the counter. He picked up the cup and looked around. The café was rather empty. One Chemist sat in the corner, glued to his screen. Another Linguist, one he didn't know, leaned against a column, looking down. A girl with long, curly black hair in a gray blazer sat in a cozy corner, staring blankly at the wall. The Man of History waved at Eddington.

"Hey, you lost? Free day, eh?"

"Right." Eddington grabbed his hot chocolate and sat across from the Man of History.

"Tell you what, man. I can't believe it. Another two months, and I'll be out of here." He crossed his arms.

"To work at The Plant?"

"Most likely. What else could we Humanitarians do? What, go blow up buildings? Those smirks in navy suits are such know-it-alls."

The Chemist from a few tables across straightened his back but soon went back to his screen.

"What is The Plant anyway? Mother is working there."

"I think it's a data entry job. To maintain L'Académie."

"Feeding the data into L'Académie?"

"As far as I know."

"So, you came here a year before I did. What was it like then?"

"Same as what it is now. Except they didn't have those annoying screens on the street. Also, not everyone wore blazers. It was quite recent that—Ed?"

"No, sorry. Just, not all were in blazers? Sorry, continue."

"There were a lot of people who didn't go to L'Académie roaming the streets. The Regime really cracked down on them recently. Called them Rogues."

"I know the Rogues." Eddington learned that term from the introductory module of L'Académie. He knew the entire Rule-Based Sequences by heart. All of the students at L'Académie did. "But what is a Double-Rod?"

"I don't know. But I know it when I see it."

"It's not in the Rule-Based Sequences."

"No, it's not. It can't be defined, this Double-Rod." The Man of History cleared his throat. "But as far as I know, this café is free from it."

The girl with curly black hair looked up and met Eddington's wandering gaze. Her eyes snapped to the table in front of her.

"But Rogues—what about them?"

"Psychos. Mad people. They were taken away immediately. I've seen a few. One was yelling on the streets a few years back. Another was sitting on the side of the street, doing nothing! Can you imagine? Out on the street, doing nothing? He was just sitting there, and his buds were off. And when a Prefect approached him, he punched the Prefect in the nose! Those two—I've never seen them again."

Eddington recalled the fate of his father.

"What happens to the people when they are taken away?"

"No one knows. I don't bother. Banished."

"Forever?"

"Yes." The Man of History finished the rest of the coffee in his cup and leaned back in his seat.

Eddington leaned forward. "Have you experienced The Cross before?"

Head tilted, the Man of History pointed at his left earbud. "With these, no."

"Well…"

"Have you?"

"No. I was just wondering." Eddington shifted.

"The Cross is dangerous. That's why checkups at The Corner are so necessary."

"I checked my buds a few days ago."

"Very good."

A Prefect passed the café door. Eddington suddenly grew uneasy.

"Yes, indeed. Model citizens." The Man of History looked at the Prefect through the window.

"Uh-huh."

"Black suits are rather slick, aren't they?" The Man of History straightened his lapels.

"Prohibited items…"

The Prefect stopped and turned his head, and Eddington met those eyes briefly. There was nothing behind his gaze.

"They had to spend many more years in L'Académie. And students like us, we don't really get to be Prefects. I think that's decided before you join The Enlightened. I think they were in another program."

"Look where they are now."

Throughout the span of the conversation, Eddington couldn't help but notice the glances the girl threw at him from the cozy corner. Eddington tried to catch the girl's eyes once again, but when he watched her, she kept her gaze trained to the wall.

"Okay, next order of business. You have gone through the Tennis Court Oath, but let's backtrack. *Cahiers de doléances*."

"Books of grievances drawn up in circulation between March and April of seventeen eighty-nine

, which contained many of the dissatisfactions of the lower estates. They wished to use the *cahiers* to inform the upper estates of necessary changes." He paid no attention to what he said, only to the girl in the corner.

"Very good! You'll run the show after I'm gone."

Eddington looked over to her again; at that moment, she turned her head left to right, inspecting her surroundings like a thief afraid of being caught.

"You good?"

"Yeah, yeah." Eddington sipped his hot chocolate.

"What were you looking at?" The Man of History turned around.

"Nothing."

The girl turned her attention back to something on her table. In her right hand, she held a rod.

"Ed?" The Man of History furrowed his brow.

With his eyes still toward the girl's general direction, Eddington said, "How did people learn? Before L'Académie?"

"I don't know. Books, maybe?"

The girl placed the rod back in her pocket and folded up the object on the table.

"Books? Aren't they prohibited items?"

"I don't know. L'Académie really is pushing learning forward, I guess."

The girl stood up. Eddington twirled a spoon in his hot chocolate, pretending to focus on the conversation.

"Enlightened society… sure is. Knowledge right at our fingertips."

"Sure thing. You—"

The girl was passing their table and bumped into Eddington's shoulder, shaking the cup in his hand. Out spilled the hot chocolate, staining his once-spotless gray blazer. The girl covered her mouth.

"Oh, dear! I'm so sorry. Are you okay?" She knelt down and inspected the stain. During that split second, she shoved something into Eddington's hand.

"It's okay. It wasn't that hot anyway."

"Sorry, then. Again." She stood up and lingered at the door for a moment before exiting the café.

The Man of History looked at Eddington, wide-eyed. "What was that?"

"Accident?"

"Look at your blazer—it's ruined!"

"I'll get it washed tonight."

"You better! Gosh, careless people. What are the likes of that happening?"

"Hmm, don't fuss. It's fine. I'll be fine." Eddington took off his blazer as he gripped what felt like a crumpled piece of paper. As he put the blazer aside, he slid the item inside the right pocket of his pants—a movement so subtle, the Man of History didn't notice.

***

L'Académie, enlightened citizens.

Please report any signs of Double-Rods found.

He kept his head down, avoiding the accusatory glare of the screens. In his left blazer pocket was the piece of folded paper. He knew if he were caught with it, the Prefects would banish him like the rest of those crazy Rogues. He looked over his shoulder again and again.

Across from the café stood a cluster of buildings. Eddington hurried down the street, turning down a side alleyway. He hoped the Prefects couldn't find him there, where garbage units rumbled like wild beasts as they compressed rubbish into compact cubes. Like every other useless thing in The Regime, trash was sent beyond The Wall.

He looked around; no Prefects lurked. He reached into his pocket and felt the texture of the paper. *This is it!* A prohibited item was resting right in his hand. He savored the feel of it. He'd known of paper, of course, but he didn't really know what it'd be like. There was even a unique scent to it, something he couldn't quite pinpoint. He had to know what was in that note. And why the girl had given it to him. And who she was. Maybe the note could help answer his questions, but he couldn't open it at The Complex: the home entertainment system watched his every move. He held his nose and hid behind one of the garbage units, taking the note from his pocket. It was a lined piece of paper with blue stripes running horizontally on the entire page and two red stripes at the top. Tear marks indicated someone had ripped it, and it was folded neatly into four equal sections.

Eddington slowly opened the folds; the page made quite a funny noise. It was a satisfying sound. He held his breath and tried to get a closer look at the faint black marks he presumed had been put there by the girl. Amongst the humming machines and the stench, Eddington was startled by an approaching sound.

Tip, tap, tip, tap.

He shoved the paper back in his pocket.

Tip, tap, tip, tap.

Slowly, Eddington arose from where he squatted and tiptoed behind a higher processing unit, barricading himself away from the entrance of the alleyway. Through the gaps of the processing unit in front of him, he saw a figure in black. Squatting down, Eddington held his breath, hoping the person would pass by.

The figure came closer to where Eddington was hiding. It was right around the corner. Full of fright, Eddington arose to look through the gaps while his right hand began to tremor again. The figure was gone. A deep breath in, a deep breath out.

"Little snitch."

A hand landed on Eddington's shoulder. He turned around abruptly; before him was the man in the long dark coat.

"Sir! I'm… sorry!"

"Hiding from the light, ye?"

"Ye?"

"Why is your blazer stained?"

"Ah… little accident."

"Accident? Oh, dear." The wrinkled man chuckled. "People are so careless today, aren't they?"

"Who are you?"

"We're not safe here. The Regime has had their eyes on you for a while." The man in the long coat looked around.

"I'm sorry, sir?"

"Things don't make sense in your head, right?" The man straightened himself. "We have to go. I know a place. Follow me."

As the setting sun cast their lengthened shadows on the garbage processing units, the two figures went farther down the alley. They were of similar height, though Eddington slouched a bit. The man in the long coat looked to his right and opened a little blue door, revealing a back-kitchen.

"In you go, princess."

"Prin—"

The man pushed Eddington through the door. "We don't have time."

The kitchen led to a wooden staircase that ascended to a living room. It was almost cheery—Eddington had never seen anything like it. Red carpet edged with elaborate patterns ran along a wooden floor, and yellow wallpaper littered with dark designs adorned the walls. His unit at The Complex was nothing like the welcoming apartment.

"We're not there yet. Keep up."

Their shoes trampled over the dark-red carpets as the man in the long coat opened the door of the unit, revealing a hallway. Windows with rusty frames illuminated the way. They continued down the hall and reached a staircase spiraling down.

"Down, kid. Quick. Follow."

At the bottom, they were met by a cellar door. The man took out a ring of keys and unlocked the padlock, and as the door swung open, Eddington felt a strange sense of familiarity. It was a small study. The only light came from a ceiling lamp that cast a warm orange glow around the room. Off to the side was a reading couch with a wooden frame and red velvet cushions. After a brief pause at the door, Eddington turned his head toward a shelf on his right. He froze in terror.

"You've never seen one before, have you?" The man in the long overcoat placed the keys back in his coat pocket. "They're books."

"Sir, they're *prohibited*!"

"And?"

"But, sir, I have to… report you." He recalled those notices on the screens.

"No." The man shook his head with the edges of his mouth raised slightly. "No, you don't."

"What if you get caught, sir?"

"I won't." He straightened himself and reached out his veiny right hand. "I'm Archer."

"Eddington." A little startled at the sudden introduction, Eddington gripped Archer's hand and gave it a limp shake.

"Yes, I know."

"I really… I shouldn't be here."

"I know." Archer placed his right hand back in his coat pocket. "Tell me now, Eddington. What happened the other day? At The Corner?"

"I was getting my buds fixed…"

"Hmm." The man took a cigarette from his pocket. "No, that's not it." He pulled out a gray lighter. The man was strange, that was clear, but the strangest thing about him was that he didn't wear earbuds.

"I…" Eddington instinctively touched the bud in his right ear. "The Cross happened."

"The Cross?" The man paused right before he was about to ignite the lighter. "Is that what they call it now? The Cross?"

"Yes. It drives people insane."

"Oh, well, well, well. You study History, don't you?" Archer lit the cigarette.

"Yes."

"What do you think History is for?" Archer drew on the cigarette and puffed.

"Mother is working at The Plant now."

"That's not my question."

"Knowing facts and dates?"

"Abbé Sieyès."

"Author of one of the founding revolutionary texts: *What Is the Third Estate*? Appeared alongside the *cahiers de doléances* throughout the Pamphlet War of seventeen eighty-nine."

"Yes." Archer slowly made his way to the couch and sat down. "Yes, yes, yes."

"Sorry?"

"Another bore." He drew some smoke into his lungs.

"How?"

"That friend of yours at the café? You don't even know his name. What else does he do other than babble? Exactly. Nothing." Smoke slowly escaped his nostrils and his mouth. Then he exhaled, pushing the rest of the smoke out of his lungs. "Do you want to know what The Cross is?"

Eddington's feet shifted to and fro; his right hand trembled.

"You've felt it before. Stuff in your head messed with your world. It changed; you started to think for yourself. That scared you."

Eddington looked into Archer's eyes.

"You still don't get it." Archer shook his head. "Kid, those buds." He pointed at the black humming earbuds Eddington wore. "What do you think they do?"

"Prevent The Cross from happening."

"Really?"

"Yes! And mine aren't working properly."

"Kid, they're working wonders." Another puff of smoke. "There's nothing wrong with those buds at all."

"Sorry?"

"Your buds. They're doing their job. They're just not working for you."

"Not sure if I follow."

A long inhale; the tip of the cigarette brightened. "Kid, people educated at L'Académie—they don't think anyway. The buds are there not to prevent The Cross. You think those in blazers are even capable of experiencing The Cross?"

Eddington stood still.

"They're just there for show." The cigarette grew shorter as the tip brightened again. "And yes, kid. How did you get here in the first place?"

"I don't know."

"They funneled you in. Tell me, do you remember anything?"

"Anything?"

Archer shook his head. "Even your memories are gone."

Eddington's entire right arm started to shake. He shoved his hand into his right pocket, and he felt the note again. He gripped it tightly in his hand as Archer dropped the cigarette butt on the floor.

"Actually, sir… I'd like to…"

"Yes?"

"Here's a…"

Banging from the cellar door interrupted Eddington.

"Prefects," muttered Archer. "Kid, the bookshelf—pull out that blue cover."

Eddington shuffled toward the shelf on his left and found the blue-covered book. As he pulled out the book, the shelf rotated, revealing a red-bricked passageway illuminated by a series of yellow bulbs. As it rotated, an orange-covered book fell off.

"Kid, take it. Run. Passage will take you to the apartment. Then get back to your Complex. We'll meet again," Archer said under his breath.

Eddington picked up the book in haste, nodded, and ran down the passage. The bookshelf rotated back to its original place, leaving the room empty of any trace of the fugitive. Slowly, Archer moved toward the heavy cellar door. He turned the lock handle and opened it. Standing at the door were two Prefects: different faces, identical expressions.

"Sir."

***

Eddington ran along the dark passage, hiding the book under his stained blazer. There was an ascending staircase at the end; he took the steps two at a time. He quickly opened the wooden door and crossed the apartment with the dark red carpet. With no time to linger, he dashed down the descending stairs and hurried through the kitchen. When he reached the garbage processing yard, he paused. There, under the noisy hums and tall shadows of the units, he finally had a chance of getting a look at the note.

He grabbed it out of his left blazer pocket and unfolded it quickly. The writing was constructed in haste, but it was still readable:

Meet me at the café when it gets dark.

A string of passing footsteps echoed across the alleyway. Eddington tossed the note into the garbage unit. The note was devoured under the constant hum of the machines. As the footsteps grew louder, a Prefect appeared.

"Sir, what are you doing here?"

"Ah, I got lost." He squeezed his right armpit tighter; the orange book was there.

"Sir, your blazer." The Prefect edged toward Eddington as his eyes scanned him from head to toe.

"Yes?" Eddington's breath shallowed. The Prefect pointed at the stained spot.

"Please get it cleaned."

"Yes, yes, of course."

"This area is restricted. Please leave."

"I'm sorry."

The Prefect returned to the streets; so did Eddington. He still walked with his eyes lowered to avoid the screens. In his head, however, those words echoed over and over.

I hate those Prefects.

Still, he dared not sound them out. One step after another, Eddington made his way back to The Complex.

"Good afternoon, Eddington," the speaker aired.

Eddington walked into the room and studied every inch of the apartment.

"Tough day?"

"Hmm? Yeah." He inspected the room. The three glass panels? Too open. The toilet? A camera in the mirror would give him away. Bedroom? An overhead camera on the ceiling kept a vigilant watch. The bathtub? Maybe.

He moved toward the tub. As he squeezed himself in, he hoped he would be out of the cameras' range. He sat there and waited.

Nothing. The system didn't speak to him for a solid five minutes. Usually, the system would attempt small talk around the clock, but it stayed silent. A few moments later, the three-paneled screens turned themselves off; the system thought Eddington was out of the house.

In the dark, Eddington slowly reached under his stained blazer. He felt the book. He couldn't believe it—he was holding a prohibited item. It had an orange cover, and a little penguin stood below the title.

"How did people learn? Before L'Académie?"

"I don't know. Books, maybe?"

He turned the book over and over in awe. *Nausea*. He inspected the title of the book. One of the few Men of Medicine dressed in a white blazer might've mentioned the term before. *Sensations of sickness with inclinations to emit fluids from one's esophagus*, Eddington recalled.

He opened the book to a random page, moving slowly to minimize the slight crackling noise of the spine. The ink gave off a subtle scent. The smooth edges evoked a string of familiar feelings. His eyes jumped over the words he couldn't quite understand as one passage eventually caught his eye: "Nothing happens while you live." He whispered the words to himself. "Days are tacked onto days without rhyme or reason, an endless and monotonous addition."

The unease he experienced on The Box with The Prefect and at the café came back in full force.

It's… an endless and monotonous addition… monotonous… in and out, L'Académic, The Box, The Prefects…

The Cross was happening to him, for sure. He had to close the book. He had to look away. Those words on the page seemed to carry powers too potent. Facts he learned through L'Académie paled in strength.

Monotonous addition… days onto days, without reason. Eddington relived those moments walking down the street, seeing crowds strolling in neat files.

He opened up the book again—despite his unease—and another passage was burned into his mind.

"I had forgotten this morning that it was Sunday."

He looked around. *Today's the rest day.* For years, L'Académie erased all conception of dates. There was only the routine: a rest day, and six days at L'Académie, then a rest day, and six days at L'Académie. Eddington kept reading.

"A cold sun is whitening the dust on the windowpanes. I am ruminating heavily near the stove."

Eddington looked over at the blinds in his bedroom. "I am ruminating heavily near the stove," he muttered under his breath. A feeling of disgust overcame him as he recalled his own morning meal. He ate it out of a silver single-portioned packet.

"Nausea…"

Sensations of sickness with inclinations to emit fluids from one's esophagus. The Medical Man's voice echoed in his head. He kept reading.

"My arms dangle. I press my forehead against the windowpane. That old woman annoys me."

That Prefect annoys me, Eddington thought.

"She goes off again: now I see her from behind. The old woodlouse!"

There he goes off again: now I see the dark suit from behind. The upright bore! For a second, traces of guilty joy overcame him. Despite the momentary relief, everything around him began to toy with his sanity. He needed answers. He only knew one fact for sure: the man in the long overcoat had muttered "hate" in his ear a few days earlier. The girl, however—he had no clue who she was. *What are Double-Rods anyway?* he wondered.

There were too many pieces that didn't make sense in his head. He opened up the book again and silently read another passage.

"The past did not exist. Not at all. Neither in things nor even in my thoughts. I had realized a long time ago…"

"That my past had escaped me." He had to sound the last bit of the passage out loud.

In his head, Archer's voice echoed:

Do you remember anything?

They funneled you in.

Suddenly, a deep disgust overcame him. He hid the book under his blazer in his armpit again and stumbled out of the bathtub. The screens in the living room turned themselves back on. Eddington struggled toward the bathroom sink. Both hands clasped the edge of the bowl as he lowered his head.

Fluids through the esophagus, Eddington thought as he retched.

The orange book, as he saw it, was similar to a potent drug—one he might have overdosed on.

My past had escaped me!

Prose lingered in his head. He dared not sound those words out. The speaker was back on: "How are you today, sir?"

Chapter 4

A broad smile appeared on the face of a young man. He wore an iron-pressed shirt and a dark-red scarf. A cup of warm tea rested on the table in front of him. Beside him sat a beautiful girl with golden hair and clear blue eyes, absently tapping the table. She rested her head on the man's left shoulder.

At that instant, the young man felt a current race through him. It shallowed his breath and widened his gaze. He had the urge to bring the girl into his arms and draw her nearer into his embrace. She was simply too sweet, too innocent to ever let go. But the young man was far too shy for such a feat. His pale face blushed as the rest of his body stiffened.

They sat in a bookstore café surrounded by titles and tomes of all kinds. The young man drank tea, while the girl had a brownie on a plate.

"Hey." The young man slowly turned his face toward the girl.

The girl lifted her head away and looked him in the eyes. "Yes?"

"I want to—" The young man stood up and grabbed the girl's hand. "Just come. I want to show you this." The two held hands and strolled toward the neatly stacked shelves of books. They were made of dark oak wood, lending a quiet atmosphere to the place that momentarily calmed the young man's heart. He slid his right hand across the book spines, his left hand occupied with holding the girl's.

"Hey." Her soft, sweet voice sounded almost like a whisper. The young man stopped and turned to look at her. With a curious gaze, she asked, "What are you looking for?"

"I—" His face softened as he blushed again. "I just—look here." He knelt down, and the girl did the same. "Here's *The Iliad* and *The Odyssey*. And wow, collected works of Ralph Waldo Emerson, and—"

"You little worm." The girl smiled with narrowed eyes. She stood back up and gently ruffled the young man's dark-brown hair. "You moth." She chuckled.

The young man lowered his head while still kneeling, concealing a smile. He pulled a book from the lower shelf and caressed the cover as he stood back up.

"This edition is simply brilliant." His eyes pretended to fix themselves on the book.

"What's it about?"

"The Trojan War, and some about the warrior Achilles."

"Exciting stories?"

"Yeah! Totally."

"You should read them to me." Her hands clasped together, and her eyes sparkled with anticipation.

"It's an epic poem; it's meant to be read out loud, though I'm not..." He laughed awkwardly as he scratched his head. "I'm not that good of an orator."

"Read them to me. I don't care." She gently placed her hands atop the young man's. Both of his hands trembled as he held the book. "Why are you shaking so much?" The girl smiled. He looked into her eyes as the two of them stood in the corridor among dark wooden shelves, holding on to the same hardcover book.

"I..."

Her voice grew faint. The details of her face began to fade. He looked over at the café's counter; a moment ago, a cluster of people talked and laughed as they waited for their orders. Now, they stood silent. Darkness crept in, engulfing the store inch by inch. One by one, they went out of his sight. He turned around and looked at his young lover.

Darkness engulfed even her.

***

Eddington opened his eyes. He was on his couch, still wearing his stained blazer. No longer was there any light from the blinds; it was dark out on the streets. He grunted—that nausea still lingered after vomiting in the sink. He tried to recall the vivid dream, but it slipped away from him bit by bit. After stretching, he opened up the blinds. Through the window, he looked out at the streets.

Day after day, an endless, monotonous addition.

Something swelled up in his chest and traveled up his nose; tears blurred his vision as the streetlamps bloated. The dream evoked something he'd never visited. He tried to remember it again, but leftover wisps of memory wilted from his mind. The girl faded, the store faded, and the momentary joy from the dream was engulfed by the darkness in his room.

He stumbled into the bathroom and stood in front of the mirror. Never once had he properly looked at himself. His hair was dark brown and neatly trimmed. His skin was pale. His frame was skinny, and his eyes were brown. He looked down at the stain on his blazer and gave off a joyless chuckle.

People are quite careless nowadays.

But something else occurred to him. He remembered the girl with dark curly hair. He remembered she slipped him a piece of paper. He remembered he was almost caught by a Prefect. He stood in front of the mirror, wide-eyed, as he recalled what was on the piece of paper:

Meet me at the café.

***

"Sir, your usual program is about to begin. Would you like to sit down?"

"No need. Thank you." He straightened up his blazer and secured the book under his armpit.

"Dinner, sir? Single portion?"

"No, thank you."

Eddington went out the door and stumbled onto the street. He had never been outside The Complex at night, and the evening wind made him shiver. The floodlights onThe Wall gave off beams of harsh white light, casting blurred circles on the ground. Masked guards armed with guns and cloaked in heavy armor stood still as statues. He looked away and walked toward the café.

Soon enough, Eddington opened the café door. There weren't many people there. A Physicist sat at a table tucked in the corner, vacantly flipping a coin in his right hand. The Man of History wasn't there; he was probably at home losing himself in the drama of the three-paneled screens. Eddington strolled to the bar and slid onto a high stool, his head down but eyes alert. There, under the dim LED bulbs, was the girl who'd given him the note. He sat next to her, but the girl didn't turn her head. Both of them stared at the bottles aligned in front of them.

"Hi." She still didn't turn her head.

"Hello."

"How are you?"

"Okay."

"Not here."

"Not here?"

"They're watching." The girl quickly glanced at the window of the café; a Prefect strolled past.

"Who are you?" Eddington's eyes were still fixed on the bottles.

"I'd ask the same question."

"I'm Eddington."

"I know," she said, tightening her lips. Her head was still turned toward the Prefect. Right after the Prefect was out of her sight, she was back to staring at the bottles.

"Why do you want me here?"

"They're watching."

"Sorry?" Eddington turned to look at her.

"Not here!" she whispered with an agitated tone. "You see that back door?" She tilted her head. There was a little blue door behind the bar. "There. You go first—I'll follow. Now!"

Eddington complied. He walked toward the back door, opened it, and entered a little courtyard out in the windy evening. He shivered and wished for the cozy warmth of the café. But then, there was a strange kind of calm in the courtyard. He saw no screens, no Prefects, just the starlit sky. He turned and saw the moon. Another sensation he couldn't describe swelled up. The moon was just there, overlooking the citizens of District-E and all the unseen excitement beyond The Wall. It hung there, unaware and uncaring, simply content to brighten the night sky.

Soon, a door slam started Eddington out of his head. He turned around and saw the girl coming toward him.

"Hey, we're safe here. It's a security blind spot." She dusted her blazer.

"Who are you?" Eddington tucked his neck in a little.

"Ada. History branch. Oh." She noticed the stain on Eddington's blazer and chuckled. "I'm sorry, still."

"No need," Eddington said with a blank face. He didn't trust her.

"You're very friendly." Ada crossed her arms.

"Yes." Eddington tucked his neck into his collar and shivered. "Why am I here?"

"For a good reason."

"And that is?"

Ada looked around, alert. Once she made sure no one was listening nor watching, she looked at Eddington with her large, dark eyes. "Don't pretend you're one of them."

"Sorry?"

"One of those people," she said as she pointed at the back door of the café.

"Students? L'Académie?"

"No, not just them." She shook her head. "The Regime, The Enlightened, The Prefects! Everything! Beyond The Wall!"

"But why?"

"You're different." She looked around.

"How did you—"

"A few days ago, when you were on The Box, what happened?"

"You were on The Box?"

"Yes. What happened there?"

"I felt unwell—sick."

"Did you know where it came from?"

"No."

She settled her eyes on Eddington. "L'Académie isn't what you think it is. And you do know why you felt sick; you know it quite well. Don't pretend you don't." Her eyes moved away from Eddington's confused gaze and landed on the bulge sticking out of his armpit. "What's that?"

Eddington looked down. He reached into his blazer and reluctantly drew out the orange-covered book.

"Oh, Christ!" Eyes wide, Ada reached for the book, but Eddington held it close to his chest. She dropped her hand. "Another one of those. What is it?"

"Nausea?"

"Interesting. You know that's prohibited? Holding on to Double-Rods?"

There it was again—that term. Everyone seemed to take the term for granted. "Double-Rods? What—what are they?"

"Really? How do you not know this?"

"I never did."

"Oh, dear." Ada shook her head. "Double-Rods. Do you know much about Physics?"

"A bit."

"Double-Rods induce a chaotic pattern, yes?"

"Yes."

"Then, imagine—" Something changed. Ada's easy-going way tensed into hyper-alertness. "Ed? Don't move."

Out of a narrow passage where they could see the streets from the back courtyard, they saw a Prefect, illuminated by a lamppost. The roaming prefect stopped at the narrow passage but didn't turn his head. Eddington's heart raced. For the first time, he realized the consequences of his actions. If he got caught for real, he would disappear, just like his father.

The Prefect stood there. Each and every second rendered itself into eternity. Eddington's right hand began to tremble. Ada slapped his arm. "Stop that." The Prefect jerked at the sound like a robot jolting from a faulty power supply, but he still didn't turn his head.

"Ed, slowly, step back," Ada whispered. The two took little steps backward, quietly, as if backing off from a sleeping lion.

"There's another passage behind us. Once we reach it, turn and run, got it?" she whispered.

Eddington swallowed. With each step toward the passageway, his breathing became shallower. His heart raced faster.

The Prefect stood still as the two backed away one step at a time. Suddenly, there was a muffled thud. The two widened their eyes and halted their breath. The book, instead of being inside Eddington's blazer, was on the concrete pavement of the back courtyard. The Prefect whipped his head around, back straight and eyes sharp.

"Now!"

Both turned and ran into the passageway behind them, Ada in the lead and Eddington following. The damp evening grass was slick and slippery; Eddington was afraid he'd trip along the way. What happened to the book? The Prefect must have picked it up—direct evidence of his crime.

"Here," Ada yelled as she pointed down an alleyway. They took a sharp turn and rushed into a store through the back door. Pursuing steps became louder and louder, and Eddington found a burst of energy somewhere deep within. Shelves full of merchandise hurtled past his vision. A door on the left side of the store was their freedom; Ada kicked it open, and they came out in a garbage processing yard. The rumbling machines were piled on top of one another.

"Up here, Ed!" Ada gripped the handles along one of the processing units and began to climb the tower of machines. The Prefect rushed out the door and saw the two climbing. "Quick!" Ada was already at the top as Eddington struggled to pull himself up, his hands gripping the edge of the unit. "Ed! Hurry!" Ada grabbed his hand, hauling him up with all her might. She was stronger than she looked; with her help, he managed to flop onto the top of the unit. A ladder leaning on the building reached the rooftop, showing them their next route. The two climbed higher and heard the Prefect climbing up behind them.

After reaching the roof, Ada pointed at the ladder. "Ed! Kick it off!"

Mustering all his strength, he gave the thing a good kick to the side; it tilted and struggled out of their sight. A split second later, they heard a string of loud metallic thuds.

"Quick! There!" They ran along the moonlit rooftop. Soon, there came a chasm between two buildings. Ada approached, lengthening her stride and leaping to the other side. Eddington paused at the edge.

He looked down at the alleyway below; the drop sent a rush of shuddering chills.

"Come on!"

"Ada, I—"

"Now!"

Eddington looked behind him, then ahead, steeling himself for the jump. Below, streetlamps illuminated small patches of ground in whiskey yellow. He leaped and glided across the gap.

"Follow me!"

Ada and Eddington reached a door set into the rooftop and descended the stairs they found behind it. Their footsteps echoed as they went deeper into the heart of the building, but there was no sign of the Prefect; they'd lost him. Still, a sense of urgency hovered in the air. Ada shouldered an emergency door open; the flickering of the exit sign hanging above it illuminated the scene. A thick film of gray dust covered the floor, and random dabs of dried white paint smeared the windows. Imposing square columns cast long shadows on the floor. The concrete walls amplified the smallest of sounds, from the slap of Ada's shoes to Eddington's wheezing breath.

Ada strode toward the smeared windows and inspected the streets as Eddington glanced back every so often at the emergency door, sure that at any moment, a Prefect would burst through and arrest them. For a few moments, the space was endowed in utter silence; Eddington could hear his own heart beating. Ada waved at Eddington and told him to come over to the windows. He walked up to her and simply looked at her with his brown eyes wide. The silence was broken eventually by a loud slam of the rooftop door caused by a gush of wind.

"Who are you, actually?" Shock and agitation bled through Eddington's voice.

"Isn't that already clear?" She crossed her arms again.

"You're from the History branch. But you're a Rogue!"

"Report me then." Ada leaned back.

"I—"

"You can't. You're also on the run."

"No!" Eddington's voice echoed. "You got me into this mess! Why did you want to meet me?"

"You wanted answers."

"Not worth my trouble!"

"For real? Open your eyes, Ed. You know something's wrong. People disappearing, dark-suited people chasing us. And look at this place! Look at it!"

Ada pushed Eddington toward the window. That nauseous sensation was back as Eddington looked down at the streets.

"I… er… endless, monotonous…" Eddington shook his head and covered his face with his hands.

Ada raised her brows. "Wait a minute." She removed his hands from his face and looked him in the eyes. "What was that?"

"What?"

"You've read a book." Ada took a step back from Eddington and lowered her head. "I see. So you *have* read some books." She crossed her arms behind her. "What else?"

"That foul old louse! Walking down the street," he recalled. "The dark-suited bores…"

"Whoa, whoa, whoa!" Ada chuckled. "Sir, you're speaking numerous prohibited items."

"I'm sorry?"

"Yeah." She uncrossed her arms as her shoulders slanted. "Not surprised. But you—you, on the other hand." She looked at him in the eyes. "How did you learn to read at all? How did you end up here?"

"Mother works at the plant, and Father was a member of District-E, but he was arrested."

"Arrested for what?"

"Don't know. Maybe The Cross got to him. He became quite mad one day and wandered out into the street. I'm not even really sure why, he never said anything to me, but he, uh—he smiled. At a tree."

"What's wrong with that?"

"Prefects didn't like it."

"Never seen him since?"

"No, not at all."

Ada looked to the floor. "Maintaining of order. Did your father own books? Or any Double-Rods?"

"That was the thing." Eddington looked down into the streets again. "What are Double-Rods anyway?"

"Oh, yes. Now, you know L'Académie wants to prevent The Cross from happening, right?"

"Yes." Eddington reached for the buds in his ears to make sure they were still in place.

"Now, what is The Cross? I bet you've felt it before."

"I was asleep one night and… I feel like what I've learned is… messing with my world."

"Yes. And that's dangerous, Ed. It isn't all sunshine and butterflies."

"I like that. 'Sunshine and butterflies.'" Eddington smiled.

Ada chuckled. "I do too. Anyway, after experiencing that mess in your head, what would happen?"

"I'd go mad."

"That's what they want you to believe. If there is true thinking, there must be things that don't quite make sense, right?"

"Yes."

"And not knowing is chaotic and scary, right?"

"Hmm, yeah."

"Right. When you are given knowledge at L'Académie, does your world change?"

"No—not really."

"Can you think with those concepts you got?"

"No. The Marquis de Lafayette, influenced by the American War of Independence, coined as the hero of two worlds…"

"Perfect recitation. But notice it doesn't mean anything to you. It doesn't relate to you at all."

"Yeah." Suddenly, something clicked. Eddington's eyes brightened. "Yeah! People don't think anyway."

"Exactly. To control people is rather easy. Give them the illusion of knowledge. Give them facts to recite."

"Yes."

"And the Double-Rods simply refer to anything that could give way to free, creative thoughts."

"Yeah, right." The nausea came back. Eddington shut his eyes and leaned against the window.

"I get it." Ada looked at Eddington and placed her right hand on his shoulder. "It'll take a while."

"What's wrong with books, then?" Eddington opened his eyes. On some level, he knew too well what books could do.

"The Regime banned them to prevent any tampering with L'Académie—books give you too much access to 'prohibited' words. And the Prefects have eyes and ears everywhere."

As Ada continued, Eddington stared out of one of the smeared windows, trying to trace the outlines of people roaming on the streets. Everything seemed to be clearer in the morning light. The view gave him a sense of elevation, like the moon hanging high above the false calm of the courtyard. On some level, he was beyond—beyond the unconscious ways of those below. A tinge of sadness lingered as he looked down. He knew he could no longer return to his ordinary ways. The truth was painful. After a deep breath, Eddington turned to Ada.

"How did you get here?"

"Oh." His questioning made Ada pause. "I got here like most. And well, my memories are muddy. But I do remember The Regime wasn't always like this. At least not when I was younger."

"What was it like before?"

"The Regime still used books at that point, but then there was a breakthrough in neuro-programming. You know, schools were slow, and children were bored. And L'Académie was born. Hard to tell. Most of the data is destroyed anyway."

"So L'Académie was a recent thing?"

"No, no, no!" Ada gave off a sudden burst of laughter that echoed. "It's just here. It's always here. How could people even tell?"

"But memories—"

"Memories don't matter! L'Académie controls your head. The Regime will just think you're mad. You're just dreaming."

From the smeared windows, something shone through. Shades of orange breathed life into the once-gray windowpanes. On the ground lay faint rectangles coming from the windows as the sun budded from the opposite building, and the space came alive with the morning light. Ada's eyes flashed with something Eddington had never seen before. She hurried to the staircase and marched onto the rooftop. Eddington followed. She pointed into the distance. "Ed! Look!"

In front of his eyes was a scene he couldn't describe. "It's... wow." Orange rays turned flaming red against the hanging clouds. The sun was tugging The Regime out of that dormant darkness. "That's..." Once again, no words came to him to help him describe the scene.

"Incredible, isn't it? Miraculous." Ada mused as she stared into the distance. Eddington was a little jealous of her way with words. The two in gray blazers stood, their eyes fixed on that distant beauty beyond the clockwork Regime. At that instant, fragments of his dream resurfaced out of the darkness. He could see himself caressing the cover of a book he once loved. He could trace the outlines of those shelves of that bookshop. Only one thing remained muddy and distorted: the girl. He didn't quite know who she was, nor could he remember her features. Maybe he was mad. For a long time, something felt real. More real than The Regime, more real than L'Académie, more real than the dramas that lulled him to sleep every night. The lapses of memories felt so much more alive than the routine he'd fallen into.

"Ed?" Ada turned to him. Her dark hair was tinged by orange sunbeams. "We should split here. Those Prefects are looking for us, and I don't want to bring on more trouble."

"Right…" Hesitant to leave behind the sunrise, Eddington walked toward the door of the stairwell. Suddenly, a thought struck him. "Ada?"

"Yes?"

"How do I get back to the streets? The ladder was kicked off. And that Prefect is probably still out there."

Ada chuckled. "You're learning. Go all the way down the staircase, and there'll be a door that will bring you to a back alley. From there, you can figure out the rest. We'll meet again."

That was what Archer had said to him earlier. *We'll meet again.* It echoed in his head. Would he ever see Archer again? Or Ada—would she get caught? How were they going to meet again?

"Go." Ada gave Eddington one last look. "Go dark. Stay dark. Still go to L'Académie today. I'll be there as well."

Eddington nodded, then entered the staircase.

Chapter 5

Eddington could hear voices come from the door leading to the outside world.

"Oi, ya bloody thing!"

"Nah, yeah. I thought that was—"

"One more. Ah! Come! You never said you had them, ace!"

"If I told you, where would the sport be? Calm your nerves."

Eddington opened the door leading to a back alley. The metallic squeaks of the hinge made the two turn their heads. They weren't wearing blazers.

"Who the hell is that?"

"I don't know. One of the Prefects?" One of them returned his eyes to the card pile.

"Pre-facts? You said Pre-facts?" The other one started laughing when looking at Eddington.

"Joe! You lubber!" the man staring at the card pile said.

"Told you!" The one called Joe returned his eyes to the card pile and laughed.

"No, you're stupid." He shook his head.

"Wait, Fred." Joe tapped Fred on the shoulder and lowered his voice a little. "He ain't got no black suit. Look'e him. And he's got crap all over his suit."

"Doesn't look like a Prefect, anyway. Too young." Fred glanced at Eddington briefly.

"Sissies in suits. Oi! You there!" Joe yelled. He had the look of a moth-eaten sweater stuffed in a closet: unkept and wrinkled. His scraggly beard aged him, but he couldn't have been more than forty, and his blue eyes radiated untamed excitement, which startled Eddington a little.

"Calm down, Joe. You're scaring him." The man named Fred laughed. Fred was more well-kept. His face was clean-shaven, and his hair was brushed. A simple white shirt with the sleeves rolled up showed a fit physique, though The Regime had eschewed exercise for its citizens long ago. The man gave the impression of an intellectual with his curious brown eyes and pale, slim face. "You, friend. Are you lost?"

Eddington stood there, searching for words.

"What'chu doin' here at the back? Weren'chu supposed to line up or somethin' today? To that, er—"

"The Academy," said Fred, his smile laced with mockery. "They all line up in suits, and off they go. Like cows to a butcher's shop."

Eddington started, realizing the rest day was over; he had to make his way back to L'Académie. He looked around, but he had no idea where he was.

"You really are lost, aren't you?" Fred smiled.

Eddington finally opened his mouth. "Yes…"

"Ha, ya smart cookies, still confused. Up in the clouds, y'all are."

"Joe." Fred gave him a side stare and heaved himself onto his feet. As the man walked toward him, Eddington tilted his head to look higher and higher. The man was tall, but there was nothing menacing about him. Joe remained seated and held on to the playing cards. "What's your name, friend?"

"Eddington."

"I see. History branch." Fred inspected the stained gray blazer. "See that door at the end of the alleyway? That metal door? That will take you to the streets. But careful—" Fred pointed at the stain on the blazer. "That might get you into trouble. It's not safe out there for you. What were you doing before?"

"I was chased by a Prefect," Eddington said. Joe lifted his head from the cards, finally focusing on him.

"Pre-facts? Those guys?" Joe's back straightened, and his eyes shined brighter with excitement. "Oh, dear. The hell you done wrong, boy?"

"Joe." Fred turned his head toward Joe. "Let the boy speak."

"I… had a book."

"A *what*?" Fred narrowed his eyes. His calm exterior began to wither.

"I had a book."

The two shared a look of shock before turning back to Eddington. "Do you still have it?" Fred asked.

"No, I dropped it."

"Ah, c'mon!" Joe threw his hands in the air.

"It's fine." Fred's head lowered as his shoulders sunk. "Where did you get it?"

Eddington didn't want the strangers to know about Archer. "I, ah… found it in an old warehouse."

"What warehouse?" the two exclaimed at the same time.

"I… I don't remember."

"What book was it?" Fred's soothing tone returned again.

"Nausea."

"Oh! You fool's boy!" Joe threw his arms in the air again. "Philosophy! Fred, can you bil'eve this chap? Lost a book o' philosophy!"

Fred took a deep breath with his forehead in his palm. "It's okay. Where did you drop it?"

"Back courtyard of the café. I think the Prefect picked it up already."

"Shame." Fred pulled out a cigarette from his pocket and turned toward Joe. "Light?" Joe set his cards down and turned an intense gaze on Fred. Fred sighed, taking out a lighter and a cigarette. He inhaled and puffed. "Kid, you don't understand. Books are the key to surviving this place." He paused and tapped off some ash.

"But…"

"Huh?"

"Aren't they prohibited?"

"Kid." Joe looked at Ed once more with those wild blue eyes. "Have you ever read a book? Do you know the eh-fects?"

Eddington nodded. He still felt sick to his stomach.

"A'l we do here, kid. We live in the dark. A'way from the suits. They wouldn't pay attention to us an'way."

"Indeed." Fred drew another inhale of smoke. "It's not often that one of you runs into us."

"Who are you people?" Still agitated and uneasy, Eddington alternated his gaze between the two strangers.

"Look'e this boy." Joe chuckled as he looked over at Fred. "The Academy, or what? L'Académie? *Je comprends pas.* How dull they are when they come outta that door."

"Please." Fred waved a dismissive hand and inhaled more smoke. "Do you really think you people in suits are all there are?"

"Yeah, kid." Joe nodded as he spoke. "Those Prefacts, them black suits, they want uh piece of us every day. Thinking we have some rods or somethin'."

"Double-Rods," Fred added. "We are about the only ones left."

"Kid, y'think that Academy thing is really helping us at all?"

"Mindless robots." The cigarette hung limply out of Fred's mouth.

Another string of metallic streaks echoing throughout the alleyway made the trio pause. The door opened. Eddington braced himself for banishment while Fred reached behind his back. Joe sat, looking almost bored. Out of the doorway came Ada. "Ed? Why are you still here?"

"Uh..." He pointed at Joe and Fred, his mouth hanging open.

"Joe? Fred? Why are you two here?"

A furrow wedged itself between Eddington's brows. "Hang on—"

"Playin' some cards, Ade. Jesus, you sound like Ma all over again."

"And enjoying a little smoke, too." Fred smirked and lifted his cigarette. "How are you, Ada?"

"Wait!" Eddington shook his head and looked at Ada. "You know one another?"

"Ha, look'ee this dullard." Joe threw his hands up and barked out a laugh.

Fred had a smirk on his face. "Joe. *Pre-facts.* Prohibited words..."

"Oh, sorry, comrade. I fergot."

Ada smiled. "Yes, these two took me in a few years ago. Without them, well, I was as good as dead." Her dark-brown eyes sparkled with mischief, and her curly brown hair flowed free behind her.

"Where did you pick up this pretty boy, Ade?" Fred chuckled, but he remained calm and collected. "You two need to go. The session for the History branch starts in an hour. Ada, you've got the thing?"

"Yes."

"Second slot? In it went?"

"Definitely."

"Ah. We'll need a spare." Fred looked at Eddington.

"And teach him how to use it." Ada nodded.

"Yes." Fred looked over to Eddington. "Ed, you'll need this before you go back in there. Or else you'll turn back into what you were before. Joe, where is it?" Joe picked up a dark-green bag and tossed it to Fred. Fred fumbled through the compartments before taking out a small green disk with golden edges. "This is our bug. On your L'Académie terminal, you'll put this into the second slot from the top. It's a disruptor, so you'll sit there and not have your brain, well—"

"L'Académie-d." Ada chuckled.

"Isn't it dangerous to bring this in?" Eddington said.

"Don't worry." Ada tapped Eddington on the back. "I'll keep an eye out."

"We need to keep you, both of you, safe." Fred sighed. "This is our only hope."

"What hope?" Eddington muttered under his breath.

"We have to go, Ed. On the street. Don't stay too close together, okay? Don't want those Prefects to question us."

"Yes... but..."

"There's no time." Fred leaned down and placed both his hands on Eddington's shoulders. "Go now!"

Eddington held the chip in his grip like a piece of stolen treasure. "Yes, of course."

Eddington walked behind Ada as she led the way. Before, she bubbled brightly with a zest for life. But once they were on the streets, she merged seamlessly into the passing crowd, wearing the same blank expression and marching the same rhythmic steps. Because she looked just like any other student in a gray blazer, Eddington was afraid he would lose track of her. He, on the other hand, stuck out like a sore thumb. If Ada was a chameleon, he was a stray donkey in a pack of horses. His blazer was stained. His eyes widened with fear. His breaths were shallow as he fidgeted with his hands. It was a miracle that upon passing a few Prefects, none had stopped him.

They continued down the path for a little while and saw Bay Seven at the station. Eddington's right hand started to tremble as he recalled what happened on The Box days before.

Endless, monotonous addition…

He obsessed over the words once more in his head as he joined the rest of the suited students waiting for the next ride to come. He glanced around at the pack surrounding him: all had earbuds plugged in, and all had the same vacant stare. A strange sense of terror seized him.

People don't think anyway…

He saw it now—what Archer had said. He looked to the opposite side of the street. It was like looking in a mirror; everything was the same.

People waited for their train ride, plugged into screens and dressed in blazers. They were carbon copies of one another. Eddington hadn't noticed before, but after seeing Ada, he realized everyone else had a gray sheen to them—as if the color had been sucked out.

But a shape in his eyeline broke the monotony of the crowd. As the winter's wind hurled along the street, the figure's long coat flowed behind him like a ripple on a river. His poise was natural and confident. His torso tilted slightly forward as he embraced the breezes of the frigid air. Eddington traced his every step, and their eyes met. Archer's gaze was piercing and convictive, while Eddington's was relieved—he was glad Archer was okay.

He wanted to cross the street to greet him and tell him everything, to share the disturbing lessons he'd learned, or maybe even tell him about Ada and Joe and Fred. But all those were passing thoughts. The Box arrived at Bay Seven, and Archer disappeared from sight.

Eddington's right hand trembled as he fell in line with the pack as they flocked onto The Box. He walked along the aisle, searching for a seat as someone behind him grabbed him by the wrist.

"Here," Ada whispered. "Stay close. Almost lost you there."

They sat next to each other. Ada's face was still as blank as the rest of the passengers. Eddington's eyes filled with agitation. The Prefect hovered at the back, overlooking the entire carriage, wary for any blip in normality. Now, that included Eddington. Each second felt like an eternity as the carriage passed by the signs on the streets. They glided past Eddington's side, but he was aware of them now. *Principles of education, L'Académie, blah, blah, blah.* Eddington tried to tune them out of his head. He stayed put in his seat like a first-time diner at a fancy hotel, woefully trying to conceal his inadequacies with precise actions. He turned his head briefly to the back of The Box. The blank stare of the Prefect confronted him. He whipped back around as Ada nudged his right foot. The Prefect stood up and walked toward the two. Eddington stiffened, his back as straight as a spoke.

The footsteps grew louder as the tall dark-suited figure came closer. Eddington reached into his blazer pocket and gripped the chip in his palm. Ada also grew quite uneasy; her disguise began to fall apart as traces of fear appeared in her eyes. The footsteps halted behind them.

"Sir, ma'am."

"Hello." Eddington's voice wavered.

The Prefect raised his right arm, his elbow remaining unbent, and pointed at Eddington's blazer pocket. "Sir." They were done. He'd find out about the chip, about Joe, about the book, about Archer—

"Sir, that needs to be cleaned." Eddington looked down as he realized the Prefect was pointing at the stain.

"Thank… thank you…"

"Is anything wrong?" The Prefect lingered.

"No. No. It's quite okay."

"Have a good day, sir." The Prefect returned to the back of The Box.

For the rest of the trip, the two dared not move. The engine hummed. As Eddington's anxiety grew, the closer The Box got to reaching L'Académie. He was going to do it. He was going to disrupt the signals reaching his head. Who was he? Just two days ago, he'd wandered along with everyone else, having discussions with the Man of History, going to L'Académie, trudging back to The Complex to be sucked into the dramas on the triple screens. And maybe he'd been living an empty life, but it had all made sense. Now, he was a Rogue, just like his father. Eddington tried to calm himself, to shove down the thoughts whirling around his brain. He didn't dare fidget, despite his anxiety—not there on The Box entrenched in The Regime. Any sudden movements would be watched and monitored.

Everyone on the ride tilted slightly forward and back, adjusting with the sudden stop of The Box. The door opened as the herd organized itself into files and streamed out of the carriage. Ada and Eddington followed the parade of people, reaching The Square where everyone was divided into their designated branches.

"Ed." Ada tip-toed as she whispered into Eddington's ear. "Remember, second slot. Security won't be able to detect the chip."

The two were funneled into single files as the herd plodded along. A security checkpoint up ahead made Eddington even more anxious; he wiped his sweaty palms on his pants. The guards stood and nodded at the detection screens. Green, pass. One gray blazer in the door. Green, another pass. Another gray blazer in the door. Everyone looked so comfortable and so at ease— like they'd been through it a million times. They were so accustomed to the flow that even the guard looked bored. Three more, two more, and one—Eddington was next.

His eyes were fixed on the indicator as his heart raced. There were too many things that could go wrong: the guard could single him out because of his stained blazer. Security could pick up on the chip in his pocket. Or the Prefect could come along and—

"Sir!" one of the guards yelled. Eddington's heart skipped a beat.

"Keep moving, sir! You're blocking the lane!" The indicator blinked green.

Eddington felt relief, but it waned as he continued walking. He followed the rest of the pack along illuminated yellow arrows on the smooth glass floor and soon reached his own cubical. He sat down, looking around for roaming Prefects. One came down from the left corridor but passed him without a glance. Another walked along the right but was facing the other way.

Eddington grabbed the screen in front of him and pretended to set up the program. A Prefect strolled past and sent shivers down Eddington's spine. His body remained stiff, and his eyes were fixed on the screen as he reached slowly into his pocket to grab the chip. He bent down centimeter by centimeter as his right hand fumbled around the terminal of the machine. The chip almost fell out of his hand a few times; the tremor of his right hand remained.

Second slot…

As he heard a string of approaching footsteps, he sprang back into his upright posture and grabbed the screen. It was definitely a Prefect coming his way. He pretended to set up the program on the screen and waited for the Prefect to walk past his cubical. But the footsteps stopped; the Prefect was right beside him.

"Sir, you need to get started."

"Ah, yes, yes." He still gripped the chip firmly in his right hand.

"Sir, your headgear isn't on." The Prefect took a step closer.

"Oh, yes." He slipped the chip back into his pocket and placed the headgear onto his head.

"Need help setting up?"

"No, no. It's quite all right." His right hand still tremored.

"It's my obligation to ensure you start on time, sir."

The Prefect wouldn't leave. There was no chance for Eddington to slip in the chip. With a tremoring hand, Eddington clicked on the screen and selected the program. The initiation button was right there on the screen; the signal was active.

All of a sudden, a loud thud came from two cubicles away. The Prefect started and looked to the source of the noise. The split second was all he needed. He took the chip out of his pocket, found the second slot, and slipped in the chip. As the Prefect turned back, Eddington had already initiated the program and closed his eyes.

Two cubicles away, a dry voice said, "Ma'am, please resume your program."

Chapter 6

"Ed!"

"Mom?" The young man looked up from his notebook.

"Come on, honey. Your cereal!" A woman with dark-brown hair stood in the kitchen. Calm rays of autumn sunshine landed on the white tiled floor, casting an air of serenity on the room. "I have to go now. You stay back and don't forget to wash the bowl," she said and smiled before turning to the door in haste. The door closed; he was alone.

The young man finished what he was writing and noted down another passage in his notebook. The cereal turned into a bowl of porridge—the once crispy bites reduced to a pot of wet paste. He didn't care. He gobbled it down and placed the remains in the sink. He rushed into his room and rummaged through stacks of books until he found one he really liked.

He placed the book and his notebook inside his satchel, opened up the window, and snuck outside. A wooden fence bordered the backyard, and a little gate led to a vast forest. Trickling streams and meandering paths created a cacophony of sounds in the woods.

He was there not just to recite his book to the birds, nor just to find a quiet place to write in his notebook, but to fulfill a promise. After roaming amongst the trees, he found a tree stump and sat down as he pulled out his notebook again to write.

"Boo!"

"Oh, dear!" He jumped, putting his hand to his chest.

"You moth!" He heard her giggles without seeing her. The girl covered his eyes with her hands. "Who am I?"

"I… hmm… I don't…"

"No!" The hands moved away. He turned around. She was in a plain sleeveless white dress. Her feet were bare, and her blonde hair flowed with the gentle autumn wind. A broad smile beamed across her face. The young man had the urge to embrace her with a hug, but he was still too shy. He gripped his notebook and stood up from the stump.

"Uh…"

She laughed. "What?" Her smile was so radiant he forgot to think. His heart beat in a rhythm as erratic as the birdsong floating down from the trees.

"I…"

She placed her hand on his; they were warm and reassuring. "Spit it out." She looked straight into his dark-brown eyes as the broad smile simmered down to something more subtle and compassionate. That was it. He mustered up all the courage he could and brought his arms around her slim waist, embracing her gently with a hug. She leaned into it, wrapping her arms around his frame. Spotty shades of interwoven branches shrouded the couple like a warm coat. Soon, they parted from the hug. The girl hopped toward the stump and sat down. "Oh! You promised! You promised!"

"Yes…" The young man blushed, scratching his dark-brown hair once more. He opened up his book and cited the first few lines.

"Yes?"

"That's what I could do so far." The young man chuckled. "It means: Sing the wrath, goddess!"

The girl in the white dress gave off little claps. "Totally a poet!" She walked toward him and reached for his left hand with her right. "Walk with me… with me…"

The young man's vision began to blur as the pressure from her hand slowly faded. The forest, the stream, her white dress—they'd all been so clear, so real. But like the tide, they retreated. The forest disappeared, as did the beautiful girl and her radiant smile. All that remained was a blue screen in front of him. He opened his eyes and felt the weight of the headset on his head. The speaker aired: "Attention all students. Your session has expired. Please make your way to the exit."

Everyone got up and marched along in single file, dressed in gray and void of life. Eddington followed their steps with a blank face and wide eyes. *That dream was real.*

He exited the building, and the grimness of the streets saddened him. He held on to the flashbacks from the dream: the woods, the stream, and the young woman. But the streets in The Regime were just the streets, endless and monotonous and gray. Everything went like clockwork, ticking on and on. Even the color bled from the world as clouds blotted out the sun.

He tried to find Ada without much success—she didn't exit through the same door. Looking for her was like trying to find a needle in a vast sea of hay. For a moment, he had nowhere to go, so he stood, observing the crowd moving on with their matters. All were occupied and busied; all were plugged in and frenzied.

He was transparent in the crowd, a ghost among the living. No one paid attention as they passed. Then again, he didn't pay much attention to anyone. But then someone caught his eye—Archer, again. Despite talking to him, Eddington still couldn't quite figure out the shape of the man. He was too mysterious, too elusive to ever pin down. Prefects watched him from their perches, hesitant and confused, eyeing the strange figure in the long coat weaving through the crowd.

Archer faded in and out amidst the suits, but there were too many questions to ask, too many things that still did not make sense. Archer glanced back at Eddington and grinned, surging even farther into the crowd. Like a well-behaved dog without a leash, Eddington followed. People surrounded him; a man bumped into him but said nothing, engrossed in his screen. Eddington continued. Two crossings ahead, Archer stood at a junction and waved, then took a left turn onto a side street void of any traffic. A sudden breeze hurled past, sending a string of shuddering chills down Eddington's back. His screen told him it was early afternoon, but the sky was dark, and the street was deserted. Empty paper containers and meal packets fluttered in the breeze, but no one would pick them up. At first, there was no sight of Archer, and Eddington sighed. As his eyes refocused, he saw Archer waving at him from an alleyway.

"Archer?"

"Kid. Up here." Archer was already at the top of the fire escape of a red-bricked building. Eddington followed and struggled up the rusty ladder. After a little lift from Archer, the two eventually ended up on the rooftop of the building.

The sky was still dark, though the night had not arrived. Rain drizzled down Eddington's face. All the other students roaming around opened up their issued umbrellas. Through the thin fog and the drizzle, their screens glowed and illuminated parts of the dark streets. From the rooftop, Eddington couldn't quite make out what the signs were saying, but he didn't need to. He sighed. Archer turned to him and nodded.

"Kid, I know."

"Know what?" Eddington turned to Archer. He'd never looked at Archer so closely before. He'd seen him, but after their meetings, Eddington could never recall the details as if he were trying to locate the memories of a dream. The man's wrinkles showed his age, but it was clear he'd been handsome at one point. His body was lean and sharp, and his eyes glittered.

"You hate this place, don't you?" Archer folded his hands behind him and took a deep breath.

"Hate is quite a strong word."

"I know it is. I know." Archer took out a cigarette. His right hand was a little shaky when he leaned the cigarette into a match.

"How did you get away from those Prefects? When I ran away from the cellar?"

"I have my ways." Archer lit the cigarette and drew. His right hand still wasn't steady, and ash fell to the ground.

"And those books?" Eddington took a step closer to Archer.

"They took them all away."

"What? To destroy them?"

"Not quite." Archer puffed out the smoke in his lungs.

"Then why?"

"These people are collectors for sure." Archer sighed.

"Right..." Eddington took a deep breath as he looked down at the street. The light rain faded, leaving the pavement a shade darker. Gloom loomed over them as the fog lingered in the air. No cars passed the little side street, but someone was stumbling around and coming toward the building where Archer and Eddington were, someone who looked kind of familiar.

"Kid, I have to run." Archer dropped the half-smoked cigarette onto the floor and stepped on it. The scarce sparkle sizzled under his foot. "They probably followed me here. I don't want more trouble."

"Archer, wait." Eddington noticed someone roaming down the deserted street. That someone wasn't wearing a blazer, and the way he strolled reminded Eddington of a vacant drunk. "Archer?" Eddington turned his head; the man was gone.

He turned his eyes to the figure again. It stumbled into one alleyway and came out another. As he came closer, he blundered into abandoned buildings and pawed through the cardboard and trash littering the streets. When he was at the foot of the building where Eddington was, the man laughed and yelled, "Kid! Wha' the hell you doin' up th'er?"

That was too loud. Eddington waved his hands around and didn't sound a word. There were probably Prefects lurking around.

"Kid! Com'on down, will ya?"

Eddington ran toward the fire escape and made his way down with clumsy moves. He managed to descend from the rooftop without much trouble. He rushed up to that yelling idiot and grabbed him.

"Joe! Quiet."

"Whoa, whoa!" Joe pushed Eddington away and held up his hands. "I ain't see nobody around here."

"No, they're watching! You shouldn't be out here!" Eddington looked around anxiously.

"Kid." Joe burst out laughing. "Look at'chu. You mean *here*?"

"Yeah!"

"You ain't got no idea of how this works." Joe pulled out a cigarette. "Why'd you think there's not them cars on'd the streets here?"

Eddington didn't answer.

"Fool's boy. This area's trashed. D'you even see them screens? Students? Them Pre-facts?"

Eddington looked around; there were no screens and no announcements around the clock. The street was quiet and cold in the light fog of a cloudy day. It was a bit too stark and bare for him.

"Boy, this place's where we'al come to scrape. Y'know? Finding something The Regime hasn't yet taken away?"

"Are you sure?" Eddington scanned his surroundings again.

"My dear s'weet Lord." Joe snapped his fingers. "Fred, come on!"

"Ed?" Fred came out of a side alley. He carried a stack of boxes full of supplies. Atop those boxes rested a few—

"Books?" Eddington's eyes brightened.

"What are you doing here?" Fred tensed as Eddington's eyes landed on the books as if he were carrying a box of sausages down a street and bumped into a stray dog.

"May I?" Eddington pointed at the stack of books.

"Yeah, sure." Joe stared at Eddington, picked up the top volume, and handed it over.

"What's this?" Eddington inspected the cover. The dust jacket was gone. All he had was a brown cover without a title.

"I don't know." Fred turned the other way to greet Joe. "Joe, found anything good yet?"

Meanwhile, Eddington flipped open the book to a random page. "I did not wish to live what was not life." Eddington murmured the words aloud. "Living is so dear... I wanted to live deep and suck out all the marrow of life..."

"To live so sturdily and Spartan-like as to put to rout all that was not life," a familiar voice yelled from behind. He turned around.

"Ada?" He was glad to see her again.

"Yes." She smiled. "Interesting book, no?"

"You've read it before?"

"Yeah. You've never read a book before you met us?"

"No, not really."

"But how—" Ada took the book from Eddington and held it up. "How are you able to make sense of this?"

"I... don't know..."

"That's very weird. It took me a good few years, but for you, it was—"

"Hey, friends!" Joe came out of nowhere, carrying a little rectangular box. "Look'ee here." He pressed a red button, and a string of unfamiliar sounds came out. It was nothing like the routine announcements from the speakers; this voice was warm and soothing, like a loving embrace. Eddington began to tap his foot and nod his head to the rhythm of the sound.

"Ya pepes know Chicago? Used to be a big, big town!" Joe gave off a broad smile. He had a few missing teeth.

"This is great." Eddington smiled. "What is it?"

Ada stood with her arms crossed. "Those two gentlemen"—she pointed at Joe first, and then at Fred, who was looking through a mailbox on the side—"played that stuff around the clock when I tried to read. It wasn't fun."

"I quite like it." Eddington smiled as broadly as Joe—though with a lot more teeth—as new sensations ballooned in his chest. He felt color bleeding into the black and white. The streets and the pavement no longer seemed so grotesque. The Box no longer agitated him. Even the Prefects didn't seem that menacing anymore.

"Joe! Look what I found!" Fred shouted, his head buried in the red mailbox.

Joe placed the little rectangle in his pocket and hurried toward Fred.

"Off rolls the head of that big fat schlub!" Fred held up what he had just discovered: a book with quite a disturbing cover.

"Are them human brains on those sticks?" Joe scratched his head.

"Joe! You don't get it." Fred flipped through the book like an eager child. "It's a textbook about the Revolution! You two! Here!"

Ada and Eddington hurried toward the two older men.

"Is that?" Ada covered her mouth with her hands.

"Yeah!" Fred affirmed along with a string of excited laughter.

"I don't get why y'all like that stuff." Joe turned and lighted a cigarette, pointing at a different book. "I like *them*, y'know. Machines, aliens, weird islands. Stories."

"Oh, Joe." Fred whacked his left shoulder. "Let us be!"

Eddington stayed quiet. His eyes were fixed on the cover. A crowd of grotesque faces stared back. Wooden piles stuck out above the crowd, breaking up the cacophony of contortion. On those pikes sat human heads.

"Do y'all know the tales of Cthulhu?" Joe raised both his hands and moved his fingers like octopus tentacles.

"Joe, we're not going through this again!" Fred snapped as laughter followed. "Don't teach them false myths."

"Nah! You don't geddet, Fred!" Joe gave off a string of excited claps. "The cosmic entity insp'red a whole bunch of things after it…"

Meanwhile, Ada and Eddington followed the two bantering men. Ada leafed through a book from Joe's pile, but Eddington's eyes were still fixed on the book Fred found in the red postbox.

"Where are we going?"

Fred turned around with that book in hand. "You'll see."

Chapter 7

After many turns and detours amongst the back allies of the streets, the sky darkened with every passing hour. The four of them looked through abandoned shops as they trailed through the windy streets. The Regime and his routine were so familiar once, so easy, but he wasn't sure he could ever go back to it. As he followed the three strangers and their charming banter, everything he'd ever known was crumbling within his mind. He envisioned going back to the apartment, attending L'Académie, perhaps even entertaining a little chat with the Man of History at the café. But the mere thought of the life he once had bred resentment. All he wanted then, as he walked the dirty streets with three strangers, was to savor the moment before it was gone. Before disaster struck. Before the Prefects caught him.

A few hours later, the sun began to set. The clouds were set aflame under reddening rays. The four looked up; all fell silent. Eddington was once blind, trapped on the same route as others. The monotonous method of

The Regime spared no space to notice the beauty surrounding them.

At that instant, Eddington's eyes brightened. The slight pressure in his ears felt rather alien. He looked over at Joe and Fred: two honest men, not afraid to live low and squalid, without buds in their ears. He looked over at Ada, dressed in a blazer just like himself. She was wearing those buds, but they were mere placebos. He looked around him: no screens hung about the abandoned corners outside of The Regime's control. People within The Regime were comfortable and orderly, utterly confined. Eddington took a deep breath—a breath he could see. He reached up to the buds and took them out. He didn't dare destroy them yet, but one day he would. Quietly, he slipped them into his blazer pocket. He could finally hear again.

"And we are here." Fred stopped in front of a little metal door and placed the stack he had collected on the floor. He unlocked a downward stairway with a bronze key. Joe and Ada rushed in the door and descended down the stairs. Eddington stood still as Fred picked the stack back up.

"Ed? What are you doing?" Fred raised his eyebrows.

"I'm afraid I'd have to…"

"No, you're coming in," Fred said.

"The Prefects will be… I haven't been at home for a while, and they have…"

"Ed." Fred placed the stack back onto the floor and placed his right hand on Ed's shoulder. "You are good with us. They have no power and no right to deny—"

"Hey, you two!" Ada's head peeked out from the bottom of the staircase. "Stop lingering. Come in!"

"Well?" Fred tilted his head toward the open door.

A loud metallic thud echoed in the alleyway. The group that roamed the streets disappeared from The Regime's view.

The hideout was so different from where Eddington lived. To the right was a kitchen with a bright blue stove and red teakettle. To the left was a living room with plush carpet. A fireplace crackled in the corner, and dark books covered a bookshelf like ivy on a building. Joe placed his collection on the kitchen counter and puttered around the place, setting up the kettle and rummaging through the cupboards. Ada was still skimming through the book as she plopped down on the green velvet reading chair. Fred was tidying up the boxes stacked near the door. Eddington saw old electronics, books, discs, and little bottles with brown liquid scattered throughout the place.

Eddington's eyes were still drawn to the book with the rolling crowd on its cover. Fred noticed it as he was sorting through the boxes.

"This?" Fred pointed to the book.

"Yeah..." Like a little kid caught staring at a stranger, Eddington struggled for words.

"Knock yourself out, kid." Fred picked up the book and gave it to Eddington. "Tell us about it when dinner rolls around."

"Wait! Why does he get to read it first?" Ada looked up from her book from the living room.

"You didn't ask." Fred chuckled.

"Well, mine's more interesting though." Ada returned her eyes to the book.

Eddington overheard the conversation, but his mind was wholly occupied by the book; his surroundings dulled and quieted. He was so engrossed he didn't pause to sit down as he read the first line of the book.

"In the modern French psyche..."

***

"Where's fool's boy?" Joe asked.

"Reading." Fred threw an empty cardboard box into the storage room.

"Where?"

"He's been talking to himself, walking around the house with that book," Ada said, her eyes still on her own book.

"My bad." Fred chuckled. "I shouldn't have given it to him."

Eddington was leaning against an upright pipe, entirely absorbed in the narrative. *The Marquis de Lafayette, the cahiers de doléances, Abbé Sieyès, Maximilien Robespierre*—those facts were no longer just facts. They were burned into Eddington's mind like moving scenes in a movie. Lafayette was restored to his lively glory, Abbé Sieyès to his fierce intellectual vengeance, and Robespierre to his shocking conviction and idealism. L'Académie's facts no longer lingered just on the surface; they were clawed deep into Eddington's imagination. If *Nausea* was a terrifying look at a grim life come true, the book about the French Revolution was an exhilarating account of revolt and the power of the crowd.

As his eyes glossed across the pages, his heart raced with the people's chants. As he met the people of the past, he recognized they were real. As tragedies unfolded in front of him, his heart churned with those who had suffered.

He looked away from the book and stared at the pipe he was leaning on. It looked strange. In fact, everything around him seemed off. The book transformed the boring days of L'Académie into times of rebellion. It made the coming days more exciting, too, to know Eddington could tear down the system like the characters did. He reminded himself he was still a student, but that seemed absurd, like the ticking clock on the wall, measuring days of inanity. He didn't know how long he'd been reading.

Soon he heard the clatter of dishes coming from the kitchen and smelled something that seemed familiar, yet he couldn't remember what it was. He followed the smell with wonky steps, as his head was still in a kind of a trance. Stories of the Revolution, of the massacres, and of the fiery speeches all lingered in his head.

"Oh! Hey!" Ada waved at Eddington as he came out of the corridor.

Fred's mouth was stuffed full of bread. He awkwardly raised his eyebrows.

"Fool's boy! Com'ere, friend!" Joe pulled out a chair and invited Eddington to sit next to him. "What'd hell you doin' in 'ere for so long?"

"I was reading." Eddington's mind was as stuffed with thoughts as Fred's mouth was stuffed with bread. The chants, the heads on the pikes...

"Well, you'll have to tell us about it soon." Fred finished his bite. He set his fork down and wiped the corners of his mouth with a napkin.

"Here ya go." Joe placed a plate in front of him and gave him a piece of warm toast with butter.

"Where did you get..." The bread, the riots, the starving peasants.

"Look, fool's boy." Joe smiled. "Gotta look whereta look; you can get most of them everything."

"Joe's a sniffling rat." Fred laughed. "Can find that kind of stuff—can smell it from miles away. Don't go scraping without Joe!"

"Oh, nah." Joe smiled and scratched his head.

"And he's a great cook!" Ada smiled.

"Nah, just them toast and butter. Nothin', nothin' cool."

"Bread," Eddington muttered.

"Huh?" Ada turned to him, her dark eyes filled with an inquisitive look.

"In seventeen eighty-nine, Lower Third Estate didn't have enough to eat."

"I know that. The seventeen eighty-eight hailstorm crisis contributed to the uproars of the lower estates. Bread riots, as they called it, were prevalent."

"No!" Eddington stood up from his seat. "People like us"—he pointed at himself—"didn't have enough to eat!"

Joe and Fred were statues frozen in place. They shared a look before turning to Eddington.

"You read that? Come on. Sit here." Ada walked up to Eddington and slowly lowered him to his seat.

"Yeah…" Eddington calmed down a little as he took out the book and placed it on the table. Upon seeing the cover, a swell of emotions flooded his senses. "But no! I didn't just read it; it felt *real*. There were things that happened before L'Académie!" His breaths were shallow. Tears oozed out of his dark-brown eyes. His right hand began to tremble.

"Boy! Stay ya nerves!" Joe grabbed hold of Eddington. "Deep, bre'th, boy! Deep bre'th."

"The Cross," Fred said, his voice grave. "If they find him on the streets like this, he'll be gone."

"We can't let that happen!" Ada looked at Eddington. Joe was beside him, holding him down.

He got it. Insanity. The Cross was insanity. Opening and devouring that book instilled images raw and explicit, immediate and gruesome, into Eddington's unprepared mind.

"Maybe he's not ready yet." Fred took a deep breath as he took out another cigarette.

"Fred, don't." Ada stopped Fred from lifting the cigarette to his mouth.

Fred paused briefly and smiled at Ada; wrinkles appeared around his eyes. "I will try."

***

"Them books are not good if you hurry too much, boy." Joe sat next to Eddington on the couch. After a few moments, Eddington regained his composure, but those images replayed in his head.

"Joe…" Eddington looked into those blue eyes. "Did it all really happen? The crisis, the famine, the peasants, and the King?"

"Out o'all, you and Ade should know them best!" Joe laughed. "L'Académie? History branch? What the hell you been doing there all along?"

"They… didn't really get to me… they were just facts," Eddington muttered. "But books…"

"I ain't get how you pepes love that history stuff so much." Joe stood up and stretched. "I like them fantasy stories above anathin' else."

"Stories?"

"Lovecraft! Verne and Wells and all, Marquez and Poe, some Greek."

"Homer?" Eddington said.

"How'ju know?"

Eddington recited the first line of the book he knew.

"Wait, what'eh devil?"

He paused in shock but said, "Nothing," and looked away from Joe's eyes. Strings of thoughts raced through his head, some cohesive and clear, others confused and muddled. Faint outlines of a forest appeared in his mind's eye, along with muddled sounds of a trickling stream. Suddenly, he turned to Joe. "What was it like before The Regime?"

"Before?" Joe sat down and leaned back on the couch. A faint smile appeared as his voice mellowed. "Kid, th'ose days—old days." The faint smile wrinkled the edges of his eyes as he looked at the bare wooden floor.

"Was it... nice?"

"Oh, f'er sure it was." Joe turned his gaze toward Eddington. "Kids li'ke you played them streets. Ha, blazers weren't a thing back then. Every one of th'em baggy p'ants walked the streets with their s'weet hearts."

"How did... how did District-E come about? L'Académie?"

"First time I saw them blazers, gosh, I was young as you." His smile faded. "A pack of 'em, walking around. Dear sweet lord, were they smart cookies. Dunno, looked like some government pro'gram thing. Then more and more of 'em began to walk the streets; fewer and fewer played and chattered."

"But... you..."

"I know, kid," Joe said, his shoulder sunken. "I ran from school when I was young. Someth'in weird hap'end. They emptied books out of libraries. Some government man came and signed a paper, took our books from home. Truckloads of 'em, gone and dis'peared, forever lost. My parents, they began to wear blazers too."

"Did they..."

"I n'ver saw them again. After a few years, some dark suit came, said I need my own living place. I ran from the backyard. I didn't want to be one of 'em." Joe sighed.

"Joe..." Eddington placed his hand on his shoulder.

"It's fine, kid." Joe raised the corners of his mouth. Those blue eyes, once zealous and wild, were filled with sorrow. Ada, wearing a nightgown, passed by the corridor and waved at the two with a smile. The lingering dark clouds of Joe's thoughts cleared. "G'd night, Ade."

"Good night, sniffling rat." She glided across swiftly, leaving behind echoes of her pleasant chuckle.

Eddington smiled as Joe looked over at the clock. "Christ, gracious. Dear, it's late. Ed, le'me show you your, uh, bed."

Eddington followed Joe. A word lingered in his mind, weaving its way with the images of the French Revolution, but it stood out more than anything he could imagine. It warmed his heart amidst all that was grim and unpleasant in The Regime.

Family.

Chapter 8

The young man had grown taller. His once-messy hair was trimmed and treated with great care. He wore a gray button-up and corduroy pants with a green cardigan wrapped around him and a satchel slung over his shoulders. As he made his way into the woods, he rubbed his hands to stay warm. He had opened the door to his backyard and trampled through the wet morning grass.

The wind was mild; he took a deep breath. The freshness of the air made him smile. He knew who was waiting for him in the woods. He walked down the path through the woods, one he'd taken so many times the grass had stopped growing. Through the damp walk and the refreshing smell of pine needles, he relaxed into nature. The sound of birds chirping filled the air. A bubbling stream chattered near him, and he closed his eyes, finding a path through instinct alone. The woods welcome him once again, and he flowed along with the breeze.

Soon enough, he saw the tree stump. It was wet, but he didn't care; he sat down. He was holding a book, but his eyes wandered to the birds, and he heard their crisp chirps assemble into a spontaneous symphony. Rays of sunlight streamed through woven tree branches, casting spotted shadows on the ground. The young man smiled.

Slowly, his eyes went back to his book. He loved reading and wanted to know the human heart intimately through those books. He flipped open the hard cover as he slid his eyes across the eloquent verses and meters.

"Amor, ch'al cor gentil ratto s'apprende…" He'd whispered the first line to himself, but soon, all verses disappeared from his sight. Slim, soft hands chilled by the fresh morning breeze covered his eyes. His palpitating heart began beating faster under his exterior calm.

"Morning."

"Hi…" The young man chuckled. "Call it off."

She moved her hands from his eyes. He turned around to see her. She, too, had grown taller over the years. The features that once carried infantile giddiness had refined into a mature and quietly confident face. In her white dress, her faint smile was mingled with a tinge of quiet mystery. Her beautiful blonde hair flowed with the passing breeze. Her eyes were still the same clear blue. He loved her.

"What are you reading now?" She made her way around the stump and sat down gently next to him. Their shoulders touched.

The young man kept his eyes on the page, but his heart was not in the rhymes nor the prose. He dared not turn toward her and look her in the eyes, but it wasn't necessary. She wrapped her arms around him and leaned her head on his left shoulder.

"Keep reading." She closed her eyes and exhaled softly.

"Of course." The young man looked up from his book into the distance. The trickling stream flowed away from the two into the thicker woods. "Actually…"

"Yes?" The girl gently unwrapped her arms and sat up, looking straight into his dark-brown eyes. The young man bent down and took off his shoes and socks and rolled up the edges of his pants. He slipped the books into the satchel and stood up, stretching out his hand toward the white-dressed girl sitting on the stump. "Walk with me."

The girl sprang up from the stump; the giddiness he knew so well bloomed across her face. She loved him too. She gripped the young man's hand firmly and strolled alongside him, trampling the grass into the thicker woods. Their bare feet pressed against the loose brown soil. Spotted sunlight danced across their faces, and a sense of calm overcame them as they breathed in the crisp morning air.

But something was wrong. Deep in the woods, the birds no longer chirped. The stream no longer trickled. The girl widened her eyes in fear and grabbed his arm. A band of men in black suits stood in the distance, guarding something. The young man looked at her; her eyes were teary. He turned his eyes to the band of black-suited men and squinted his eyes.

"What—" the girl whispered.

"Quiet!" The young man brought her closer to him as they moved a little closer to the band of men. They stood orderly and neatly. They all had some kind of earpieces, and they remained alert and poised.

"Ed…" The girl leaned closer to the young man.

"I know." He held on to her tighter, but his eyes were fixed on one of the men. They were so orderly and so—

Snap. The black-suited men all started at the same time. The girl trembled in his arms. One of the men turned his head and looked straight into the young man's eyes. He stared back. Those eyes were so hollow; that posture so upright.

"Ed!" She looked up at him.

The woods brightened. The men disappeared in a flash. What they were guarding deep in the woods, no one really knew. Soon everything was bright, and she was gone. Nothing but a voice remained.

"Ed!"

"I know... I know..." Eddington opened his eyes in a room. Ada stood alongside his bed and was looking at him with her arms crossed. He was still dazed from a night of sleep. The room looked alien—as if he'd woken up in another dream. He glanced around, trying to adjust to his surroundings. The room was quite simple, occupied by one bed, a desk, and a nightstand. He looked at Ada. She stood with her arms still crossed and her eyes narrowed.

"Yes?" Eddington sat up from his bed.

"You talked. In your sleep." Ada raised her brows.

"Really?"

"Guess who sleeps next door?" She took a step closer to him.

"I'm sorry..."

"That didn't sound like anything I know. What language was it?"

"I have no idea."

"Careful now—that could get you arrested." She made a gesture across her throat and slowly walked toward the door. "Get dressed. L'Académie starts pretty soon." She sounded smug—like she knew something he didn't. He felt like an idiot.

He stood up from his bed and tidied up the blankets. He dressed himself up in his shirt and his trousers. He was ready, but he was missing his blazer.

"Hey, Ade?" Eddington leaned his head out his bedroom door. "Where's my blazer?"

"It ain't cleaning itself, boy." Joe appeared in the corridor. "Here it is fer ya."

"Oh." Eddington walked out of his room and saw Joe standing in the corridor with his blazer. The stain was gone, and the creases were straightened. He took the blazer and smiled at Joe. Joe nodded and went back to the kitchen.

"Come on. We have to go." Ada made her way up the staircase of the hideout. It felt so natural. It felt like they were just going to school. It didn't make any sense.

***

The session at L'Académie was standard and uniform. They took the same ride on The Box and went through the same procedures to get into their cubicles. Eddington wasn't scared of the Prefects anymore. He was more and more able to hide away his interior as he, too, blended into the flowing crowd, orderly and steady like the rest.

At the end of the session, Eddington was amazed he was able to find Ada at The Square at all. They walked alongside one another but didn't dare talk. Amidst the crowd, Eddington thought about Archer again. He thought about his previous encounter when he led him away from the crowd into that dirty side street. As Eddington and Ada walked through The Square, all they could see was a solid crowd of gray. Different colors bled into the roaming crowds the farther they got from the entrance of L'Académie. Eddington's eyes caught someone in a brown blazer, but he quickly looked away. A Prefect was roaming alongside Eddington and Ada, but he didn't seem to notice anything. They were almost out of The Square when a hand suddenly landed on Eddington's shoulder.

"Hey, what a concept." The voice sounded familiar.

Startled, Eddington turned around; it was the Man of History. The roaming Prefect came over. "Sir, please hold conversations elsewhere."

"Thank you." The Man of History turned away from the Prefect. He whispered to Eddington, "You know where to meet me," and disappeared into the crowd.

Never before had he noticed that strange quality of the Man of History. But as he looked around him, he noticed it wasn't just the Man of History. Everyone in The Regime behaved the same way: there was a strange cheerfulness toward compliance. The Man of History did not fear the Prefects, nor did the rest of them. They were content, and they knew there was no reason for the Prefects to arrest them.

Ada nudged Eddington on the shoulder. "Careful."

He entered the café with Ada and was greeted by the Man of History.

"Hey, my friend. How do you do?"

"How do you do?"

"Perfect." The Man of History set down his paper coffee cup. "What else have you learned?"

Eddington searched blankly in his mind space. He didn't learn anything. The chip interrupted the signal from L'Académie.

"Uh, The Terror."

"Reign of Terror, eh?" The Man of History smiled and took a sip from his cup.

"Robespierre," Ada added. "He was considered as one of the main advocates of The Terror along with Danton and Marat."

"Let us be terrible so the people don't have to!" Excited by the recitation, the Man of History stood up and performed a salute. But then he turned toward Eddington.

"What happened to you? Dull and quiet now? Are your buds—"

"Yes! They are." Eddington took a step back. He didn't want the Man of History to know he took his buds out. The familiar feeling in his stomach came back, and his right hand started shaking again. Ada noticed what was happening tapped him gently on the back.

"Was it—yes, it's you!" The Man of History recognized Ada. "You spilled coffee on this guy!"

"Yes." Ada just looked at him.

"History too?"

"Indeed."

"October days?"

"Mass riot as a result of The Great Fear. People were starving as rumors of grain hoarding agitated the people. King Louis the sixteenth was marched to Paris from Versailles."

"Brilliant!" The Man of History clapped. Eddington couldn't take it anymore. He couldn't stand the café or the Man of History, nor the talks filled with nothing but empty facts and pure orthodoxies. The man caught facts like a dog playing fetch, delighted by nothing more than his own arrogant stance.

"Excuse me." Eddington walked out of the café with his jaw tightly clenched.

"Later." Ada gave the Man of History a slight side glance and went after Eddington.

"What were you—"

"Not now." Eddington placed his hands in his blazer's pockets and walked down the street while looking at the ground.

The two stayed silent. Eddington walked in front, and Ada followed. Soon enough, they were at the entrance to the garbage processing yard.

"Ed?"

"I have to… go somewhere. Ada, go home." He straightened his lapels.

"But, Ed." She took a step closer to him.

"No, you're going home." The word *home* carried such a strange ring.

"What are you—" She looked at the garbage processing yard, then turned back to him. "That's a restricted area."

"I'll tell you later. I need to…" He saw the little blue door leading to the kitchen.

"What is it then?"

"Go home." Eddington backed away from her.

She tilted her head, a deep furrow forming between her eyebrows. "Stay safe."

He'd arrived in that carpeted apartment after going through the kitchen and climbing the stairs. Soon enough, he reached the descending stairwell leading to the cellar where Archer lived. He went down and knocked on the cellar door.

Nothing.

He knocked again, still nothing. A string of fleeing thoughts went through Eddington's head. Was he captured? Imprisoned?

"Archer?" Against his own instincts, he yelled as he knocked again. Still nothing.

At that instant, footsteps seemed to linger above the staircase. The tips and the taps, so orderly and poised, startled Eddington. He looked around fanatically for a way to escape to no avail; the locked cellar door was all there was. The footsteps descended the stairs. They sounded too familiar, too orderly and mechanical to be anything else. Mustering all his strength, he kicked the cellar's wooden door. The loud clanging of the metal accelerated the mechanical footsteps. Another kick, to no avail. Those quick steps grew louder. "Sir?"

He could hear the Prefect stalking down the stairs, only a level away from Eddington. In a moment of panic, he twisted the doorknob, and the door swung open, revealing a cold and deserted room. Eddington could hear the Prefect move behind him. "Excuse me, sir." The Prefect noticed the open door and rushed toward Eddington. His eyes met that hollowed gaze for a split second. In haste, he slid into the room and slammed the door shut. The once clear shouts of "sir" were muffled by the wooden door, and the room was pitch black.

Eddington stumbled across the deserted room. The banging at the door grew louder and more impatient. He tripped on a chair and fell, grazing his palms against wooden splinters coating the floor. The banging stopped. Eddington grew more uneasy. He was frozen in place as his palms oozed blood, unsure what to do with the sudden stillness in the room. He stood back up and swept his hands across the empty shelves, disturbing dust as it puffed up in the air.

At last, after leaving traces of his blood across those shelves, he felt the lever. The shelf turned, revealing a dark passageway. He stumbled in and ran through the passageway. His elbows bumped the walls, and he clenched his jaw. Finally, he reached the staircase that led to the carpeted apartment. Eddington collapsed as he left red handprints on the wooden floor. In a fit of utter dismay, he threw up. He felt as though the place was eating him away. It was way too much. He realized he could never go back to The Regime. He could no longer fit back into the ins and outs. He could never be that person who goes home and watches the screens. He could never, ever entertain another chat with that Man of History or any of those goons at the café. He was cynical and hateful. Cynical of the utter unconsciousness. Hateful of the ignorant bliss.

He got up and went out onto the balcony of the apartment overlooking the empty streets. He left two bloody handprints on the rails of the balcony and stumbled back to the apartment. The world began to spin around him; nothing seemed real. He stumbled down the stairs to the kitchen and struggled even to walk. He clasped his hands together to ease the pain, but it hardly did anything. Blood was oozing between the finger gaps. His vision slowly faded as everything gradually darkened; that time, it wasn't a dream. He pushed the kitchen door open, once again leaving two red handprints, and collapsed into the alleyway. His vision blurred, and the hums from the garbage processing units grew softer.

He turned his head and squinted against the sun. A dark figure appeared in the distance.

"Sir?"

With the last of his strength, he got up and attempted to run, but his legs were no longer under his command. He collapsed again as he left behind traces of his blood on the ground.

"No." He kept crawling, trying to get away from the figure.

The humming grew quieter. His breathing grew heavier. He got up again, but it was nearly impossible to stay his gait.

"Ed?" A voice, familiar yet distant. His fading awareness could not bring up who it was. "Ed?"

The figure rushed over and grabbed Eddington's shoulders. Eddington fainted and fell. The humming from the garbage units went mute.

Chapter 9

Something felt off, though everything seemed the same. The chirping birds and the trickling stream harmonized in the pale afternoon light, just like any other day. But he couldn't get the men dressed in black out of his head. They made him so uneasy he couldn't read. His eyes merely drifted across the ink markings on the page, and the usual joy he felt from walking in the woods was replaced by a hint of worry. He tried to dive back into the book, but his wandering mind refused to concentrate. A little later, those arms wrapped around him from behind. Her chin rested gently on his left shoulder.

"Hi," she whispered into his ear.

He stayed quiet. She walked around the stump and sat next to him. "Are you okay?"

He closed his book and took a deep breath. "Something's going on… something's not… something's…" He looked into the distance as his right hand tremored a bit.

"You mean those people in suits the other day?" She looked at him with concerned eyes.

"No, not just that." He squinted, trying to organize his whirling thoughts.

"Then what?"

"Can you see that right there?" He pointed into the thicker woods. The other day, it was only a metal rim guarded by the men dressed in black. The rim had turned into a gray capsule with a door. His hand tremored some more.

"What is that?" She covered her mouth and widened her eyes.

"I don't know." He shoved his hand in his pocket.

"What are those men in suits?" She turned to him again.

The young man took a deep breath. "Whatever they are, there's something... weird about this thing."

He turned to her. She was the girl he loved. He'd always known her as sunny and vibrant, but her wide eyes were full of fear. The young man leaned over to her and brought her into his arms.

"It'll be fine."

"Are you all right? Your hand is—"

"I'm fine." He tried his best to steady his hand.

"Did people come to your house?" Her hand reached out and touched his cheek.

"Yes." The young man closed his eyes and sighed. "They took away some books. Not all of them, but enough."

She leaned closer to the young man and closed her eyes.

"It'll be fine." He brought her nearer and kissed her on her forehead. "It'll be fine," he whispered.

A ray of sunshine broke through the thin cloud, shining in the girl's blonde hair. He held her near, but he felt like he was losing her. The trees faded away with the trickles of the stream. What remained was the warmth.

***

Eddington slowly opened his eyes. He was wrapped in layers of old rags, and his hands were bandaged. There was a barrel next to him; flames rose from it, warming him. He had no idea where he was, and no one was there to give him an answer. For all he knew, someone was near, but the barrel only illuminated a small patch of ground around him.

Footsteps echoed around where he was, but he wasn't scared. They sounded familiar: a moderate pace with a graceful ring.

"Ed! You're awake!" Fred came into the illuminated area as he dumped some scraps of wood into a burning barrel.

"Fred… where…"

"Shhhh!" Fred hunched his back and looked left and right. "They're probably still around."

Eddington paused for a second in silence. Fred listened intently to every little sound around them. After making sure no one was around, he sat down next to Eddington.

"What were you doing?" Fred whispered.

"I was—"

"Being an idiot!" He stood up and paced around. "What were you thinking? You could've died, or one of them could've arrested you!"

"I'm sorry." Eddington clutched those rags closer. It was quite cold out at night in The Regime.

"Ade came back and said you were up to something."

"Hmm."

"And I came to have a look. Christ, there you were on the ground."

"Hmm."

"Did you know how much blood there was? Christ. You were all over the place. Did you know? How did you cut your hand?"

Eddington looked down at his bandaged hands and smiled.

"Fool's boy?" Fred knelt down, trying to make sense of the smile.

Eddington busted out laughing as Fred flinched. "Quiet!"

"Sorry…" Eddington tried to restrain his laughter. It was a jolt of some twisted joy. "Where are we, Fred?"

"Side district." Fred paced around the barrel some more.

"So, no Prefects around?"

"A few." He said as he pulled out a cigarette and lighted it with the edge of the barrel's flame.

"Didn't Ada—"

"Shhh!" He placed the cigarette in his mouth. The tension on his face eased at the instant he inhaled. He stopped pacing around. His steps slowed, and his eyes grew calmer.

"What are we going to do now?"

"We'll stay for a bit. Just a bit. Then we have to move. Those bastards are patrolling the side districts now."

Eddington looked at the flame coming out of the barrel. In his head, he had a thousand more questions to ask. He wrapped the rags tighter around himself as a shot of breeze hurled past the side street they occupied, wavering the flame.

"Fred?"

"Yeah?" Fred was back in his element after the smoke.

"I keep having this weird dream." Eddington looked at the ground.

"Oh? What about?"

"It's been like this for a while now." Eddington took a deep, cold breath. "It's always a dream in the same place."

"Oh?"

"I was in a forest with a stream, and…" He paused as a wave of sadness overcame him for no apparent reason. "I don't know what it was."

"Oh!" By then, Fred was completely fixed. He stood there like a calm intellectual. "Well, Ed. L'Académie, we all know it's—problematic." He drew some more smoke and puffed. "Maybe you're experiencing some flashbacks. Maybe it's real?"

"You mean…"

"Hmm." Fred screwed his brows for a split second and continued: "You know, it's hard to tell. How do you know if the past was real? L'Académie likes erasing things from your head."

"Like?"

"Memories and all."

Archer's words came back to haunt Eddington: *Do you remember anything?*

Not just the words—he recalled those uptight stances of the Prefects: they were perfect. Perfect cogs in the machine that was The Regime, emotionless and efficient.

"But why am I…"

"Ed." Fred knelt down. "Be frank with me. Just who are you exactly?"

"Huh?" He was caught off guard by such a sudden question.

"How were you able to understand those books when you read them? Took Ada years. And the other night, she caught you speaking some other language when you were asleep."

"I don't know." He recalled the muddy memories of his dreams, but they were too distorted to understand.

"Right." Fred stood up and looked at Eddington with that strange regard in his eyes. He dropped the cigarette butt on the floor and smothered the spark with the bottom of his shoe. "Time to move. We can't stay here for too long."

Fred helped Eddington up and extinguished the flame. The backway was plunged in darkness. Fred took out a torch and helped Eddington through a door.

"This way."

They went along some of the same backstreets and traveled through more random doors that all looked the same. Eventually, they met up with Ada and Joe in another back alleyway.

"Ed!" Ada rushed over to the walking carpet wrapped in old rags and hugged him. "I thought... I thought you were—"

"Told'ya he's a damned fool. Gaud, did'ya know how dangerous it was?"

"You idiot." Ada looked into Eddington's gaze with her dark eyes. "Never again!"

"Jesus, mama Ade." Fred tried to talk like Joe. "Ain't we safe now he're?"

"Fred ya'bastard. Stole another smoke?" Joe narrowed his eyes as he looked at Fred. Ada turned and looked at Fred with an angry stare.

"Whoa. Calm your nerves. It was just a…"

"Just a smoke?" She crossed her arms.

Eddington's attention floated away from the chatter. Far across the darkened alleyway, a figure passed under the dim streetlight. Eddington took a deep breath. He knew who it was. He wanted to rush up to him and talk to him and tell him about the ransacked cellar, but he was too weak even to walk on his own.

"Ed? What'chu lookin' at, friend?" Joe looked toward the other side of the alleyway. Archer wasn't there anymore.

"Nothing." Eddington's eyes were fixed on the distant darkness.

"Archer…"

He wanted to see him so bad it became somewhat of an obsession. He needed answers, and if anyone had them, it seemed Archer would. Why did The Regime collect all the books? Where was that forest in his dream? Also, who was that girl?

He was alone in his room as he ruminated over those thoughts. His hands felt better with the bandage, but he still felt sick in the pit of his stomach. In the living room, the other three were entertaining themselves with books and a little music. A jolt of sadness came to Eddington. Maybe he couldn't even relate to those people. Was he like them, or was he doomed to loneliness? Maybe they only wanted to survive; maybe they didn't want to know.

"Ed!" Ada called out. Her voice was muffled by the door. "Come here!"

Eddington reluctantly got up and exited his room. Ada was sitting on the carpeted living room floor, reading a book. "What were you doing in your room?"

"I was… thinking."

"Sir." Ada sat up straight and pretended to talk like a Prefect. "You spoke of a prohibited item!"

Eddington smiled.

"Fred and I were talking about you. Just how are you able to pick up a book and read it? Most of those words in the books were prohibited according to the guide."

"Yeah, I told him that. It's strange." Fred looked over from the kitchen. "It took you years, but for him, it was like *that*." Fred snapped his fingers.

"I don't know." He sat down and picked up a book lying on the floor.

"You're quite strange." Ada chuckled. She returned to reading her book.

"Hmm." Eddington looked at the book he had picked up.

"I first met Dean not long before my wife and I split up."

"Which one is that?" Fred looked over from the kitchen.

"Cover's gone." Eddington held up the book.

"I don't know." Fred went back to his kitchen deeds. "Picked it up about yesterday. Haven't read it."

"Hmm…" Eddington kept on glancing at those words.

He was in his room for hours. Wild adventures took over his senses and expanded his world. If *Nausea* was a grim life come true, the book without a cover was a manifesto to rush out and, as Sal Paradise in the book would've liked it, "grab life by the balls." He was drawn to the stories and weird encounters as the characters traveled around "the United States." It was incredible, unlike anything he'd ever known. After a few more pages of reading, he had a sudden urge. He knew it could be done. He knew there was no way he could deny that feeling.

"Ada?" Eddington went out into the living room again. "Do we have pieces of paper?"

"You're quite mad," Fred said from the kitchen.

Ada didn't say anything as she crawled over to the bookshelf. There were three drawers below the shelf. She opened one of them and took out paper and a pencil. Eddington grabbed them and nodded as he rushed back into his room.

***

"Where's fool's boy?"

"He was in there for a while."

"The hell's he doin'?"

"He wanted some paper and pencil, I gave it to him, and now"—Ada glanced at Eddington's door—"he... he's lost it."

No one could ever reach beyond that door. Eddington was mad. He sat as he poured words out onto the page. One sentence after another, one paragraph joined by another. There were things he couldn't quite describe out loud, but they came to the page with ferocity and conviction. He wrote about The Regime, The Prefects, the prime winter, those books that disappeared, and his twisted dreams. It carried such a thrill, such a zeal, that it filled him up with childlike delight. He continued writing page after page. The dulling tip of the graphite pencil rendered the strokes thicker and thicker. The papers, once blank, were filled with squished paragraphs. It felt incredible.

"Ed, what's—" Ada stared at Eddington, wide-eyed.

"Are you—" Fred ran over to Eddington and snatched the pages from him. "What have you done?"

"Wha…" Joe couldn't even find the right words to speak.

"If they find him—" Fred gave Eddington a side stare. "We're all done. All gone."

"How?" Ada was still wide-eyed. "Where did you learn to write?"

Eddington shrugged.

"Le'me have a look." Joe took the pages from Fred. He, too, widened his eyes. "Boy, you mad."

During dinner, no one spoke as openly as before. Everyone cast weary stares at one another. Movements, once natural, became quite rigid. The only one at ease was Eddington. It was a strange feeling. For the very first time, he was content.

"Ed? Another piece of toast?"

"Yes, please." There was a genuine smile on his face.

"Welcome." Fred reached for the bread, his movements rigid, and settled it on Eddington's plate. Joe, on the other hand, stared at his plate with narrowed eyes.

"Baked beans?" Ada offered.

"Oh. Thanks, Ade."

"Welcome."

He felt the shift in mood, and it made him a little uneasy. He felt an urge to lock himself up in his room again.

"Ed?" Fred took a deep breath with his eyes squeezed shut. "Just who are you exactly? Be honest."

"I'm from the History branch, like Ada."

"Sure, you are. But how do you explain reading and writing? It's impossible what you did."

Eddington stayed quiet.

Fred stared at him and shook his head. "Not in that short a time."

"Why not?"

"I've not seen it before. You shouldn't be able to read. And writing?" Fred scoffed. "No way, absolutely no way. Not after L'Académie."

"And they'all damn good as'ell." Joe chimed in. "Gaud, where'ja get them words?"

"They came to me."

"You're mad." Ada gave a dry chuckle, but the tension in the room remained.

All Eddington could hear was the sound of utensils striking plates and cups. His uneasiness grew. He felt as though they no longer trusted him, and he could no longer trust them. Suddenly, something came to him. The disappearing books, the capsule in the woods, his beloved, L'Académie, and those Prefects...

"Fred." Eddington looked up from his plate. "Where did all those books go?"

"I don't know." Fred concentrated on his plate.

"Prob'ly burned them." Joe examined his nails.

"The books we have are the only ones left. If they find them, they'll take them too." Ada was the only one who looked Eddington in the eye.

"Fred." Eddington's eyes were still fixed on him. "Could it be they stored the books somewhere? All of them?"

"N'ah. No lib'ry could store so many books." Joe rubbed his palms together.

"And why would they do that?" Fred shook his head.

"Preserve the old? I don't know..." Eddington said.

"There's no point." Fred set down his utensils.

"As an archive?" Ada sat up a little straighter.

"There's no point." Fred pulled out a cigarette.

Chapter 10

He needed to find Archer.

Eddington stayed in his room for days. On certain nights, he heard murmurs beyond his door in the living room. He tried to eavesdrop on their conversation, but the only words he could make out were "trouble," "danger," and "caught." His only focus was writing, and his scribbling wore away the pencil so much he had to sharpen it with an edge of the dark-red brick wall. Sometimes, he went out on the streets for casual strolls, but he spent many a late afternoon alone in his room. He still attended sessions at L'Académie, but they were just routines for him to follow. Every day, he traced swiftly through the monotonous crowds, confident after the thrill of writing. The Prefects no longer scared him, either.

The café, which he did visit a few times, was the same café, but being there felt a little different. One time he became aware of a scent he never paid attention to and later realized it was coming out of his cup. Occasionally, the Man of History greeted him during his visits. For some reason, Eddington no longer hated the man; he found himself wondering why he ever did in the first place. After a few long chats on certain days, Eddington almost looked forward to their little catch-up at the café. He was like a mere rambling fool, and there was nothing wrong with hanging out with fools.

The source of his joy came from the room he occupied alone. Under the dim lamp, his pencil shortened as pages were filled. He went to bed each and every night with a smile no one could see. Writing liberated his tangled thoughts.

He took a deep breath.

"Ed." Ada opened his door. "Dinner."

Pockets of acceptance felt rather weird coming from those three; they were ridden with suspicion. At the dinner table, all of them stared down at their plates and glanced at one another wearily.

"Joe, another piece, please." Fred didn't look up.

"Sure." Joe passed the plate full of toast to Fred, though he kept his face trained on the table.

There was a seal, some thin film of silent agreement no one wanted to breach. Eddington accepted it.

"Ed?" Ada turned to Eddington, looking him in the eyes. "Where were you in the morning? Out there?"

"I met a friend at the café."

"Of course," Fred muttered under his breath and took a sip of water.

"Why didn't you tell us?"

"It was that one you've met before. The Man of—"

"You know it's dangerous for all of us, right?" Fred raised a clenched fist, his fork suspended in midair as he pointed his finger at Eddington. "If you get caught, you know what would happen, right?" Chunks of food flew out of his mouth as he spoke.

Eddington nodded, though he didn't know. Maybe Fred didn't either.

A window of silence. Joe got up, placed his plate in the sink, and opened up a kitchen cabinet.

"We're runnin' out," he muttered. "Have to do anoth'r scrape… Them bastards are more and more strict now." He sighed.

"How so?" Fred asked.

"I was tailed by one of 'em. Them black suits. I think they know who we are but not where we are. Gotta be real careful 'round here."

"Damn it." Fred drew a long deep breath and instinctively reached into his pocket.

"Fred, don't." Ada stopped him again. "You promised."

"Damn right!" The hand that reached for the cigarette tremored, suspended between guilt and his impulsive mood. "I—damn. I'm sorry." The impulse took over; two fingers grasped the cigarette. Fred held it up to his mouth and lit it.

Eddington sat still. He looked at Fred as the tension on his face dissolved with each draw of the cigarette. The once assured façade of calm in Fred's eyes dissolved with the tension, leaving a broken man before Eddington. Outlaws, Eddington thought, people who lived in the hidden cracks of The Regime, were just a batch of clueless bands capable of random bursts of rebellious efforts that went nowhere. He thought about Archer again, his swift figure strolling amidst the crowd, and another string of thoughts followed: the girl in the white dress, the pretty stream, the deeper woods.

"Ed." Fred puffed out the smoke in his lungs. The room looked a little hazy. "These Prefects and the surveillance. If we make one wrong move, we're gone."

"I understand," Eddington replied in a monotone. He picked up his plate and placed it in the sink. He went back to his room and sat back down at the desk.

The tip of the pencil dulled, and the length of the pencil shortened, but he had to keep writing. It was his only source of refuge in the sea of monotony, in the sea of people dulled by facts. Without the pieces of paper and the pen, what was left? He felt like he was drifting away from everything as he produced those pages. L'Académie was just a part of the routine. Ada no longer said hello to him in the morning; instead, she regarded him with concerned eyes. Fred and Joe, day by day, seemed to lose the quirky charm of aging boys. Paranoia gripped them tight.

He didn't listen to Fred's warnings. Their pain and their fear were his no longer; he felt numb to it. Eddington simply strolled down the streets on some days, observing everyone's comings and goings. People still walked in straight lines. They were still glued to their screens with earbuds as they rode The Box. They still separated into neat files at L'Académie. The routine of The Regime was a clockwork art.

Walking down the once-dull streets, Eddington realized he no longer belonged, and it was okay. He felt outside of every interaction around him, yet he was involved too. The same old café stood in front of him. People sat in comfortable chairs and enjoyed their drinks and chats. A pair dressed in blazers sat on the street curb: a boy in brown and a girl in gray. They were next to each other, but there was also a degree of separation, like they didn't want people to know they were together. They stretched out their hands, trying to reach the other. Eddington stopped and looked at them, and they jumped, scooting apart. He took a turn at the junction and walked into a shop with shelves of food. Through one of the shelves, he heard fragments of a conversation from a neighboring aisle.

"Two more years, and I'll be out."

"Oh, you're lucky. You excited to see what's beyond that big wall?"

"Yeah. This Chemical Engineering faction really did just…"

"Ah, yeah, that's very…"

"You?"

"Faction… Linguistics… years, three more? I lost track. I'll be fine."

"The Plant then?"

"Hey, don't you… The Plant… Ever heard of that… It's…"

A string of laughter followed that conversation. Eddington chuckled and walked out of the store, meeting a Prefect head-on.

"Good day, sir."

The Prefect looked at him with those expressionless eyes and walked away. Eddington nodded. At least they were polite. He wandered back to the café and saw the Man of History sitting in his chair, staring into space. The window was fogged amidst the early afternoon chill. Eddington pushed open the door.

"Ed!" The Man of History stood up.

"Hi—um." Eddington paused. He'd never know the man's name and never bothered the ask.

"Hi, um?" The Man of History mimicked him, tilting his head. "Stop lingering there, will you?"

"What's your..."

The man was even more confused.

"Only remembered you as the History person." Eddington shrugged.

"Ah! There we go. The name's Thomas, but you can call me Tom. How could—"

"Common Sense?"

"Paine? Thomas?" Thomas's eyes glowed.

"Yes."

The Man of History—Tom—cleared his throat. "A revolutionary pamphlet by an English man published in seventeen seventy-six eventually played into the drafting of the Declaration of Independence on July the fourth of seventeen seventy-six."

"Perfect." Eddington smiled. Maybe plugging himself back into L'Académie wouldn't be that bad.

He could hardly remember what annoyed him so much before.

"Ed? Something old." Thomas sat down on his chair.

"Yes?"

"Bailly." Thomas took a sip out of his cup.

"Oh, the astronomer. Got his head chopped off during the Reign of Terror in seventeen ninety-three."

"Twelfth of November, seventeen ninety-three."

"Ah, yes." Eddington scratched his head.

"What happened to you? Not quite as sharp?"

Eddington smiled. "L'Académie hasn't been good to me."

"Well, get it checked out."

"Maybe I will." Eddington took a step back. He hadn't been wearing earbuds, and he didn't want Tom to see. Through the foggy window, people walking past the café looked like bloated watercolor figures. Blobs of navy blue, brown, beige, and black all passed them by. Some were big, and some were small, but all walked with the same rhythmic steps. Eddington and Tom both gazed out the window as if appreciating some work of dynamic art. Among the passing figures, one made Eddington sit up straight—Archer. He stood in view, refusing to leave, and a familiar yearning came back to Eddington.

"Excuse me, Tom." Eyes still fixed on the fogged figure, Eddington turned and walked out.

"Later." Tom's eyes were also glued to the fogged window. The man melted away from the view, making sure Eddington saw him first.

Eddington pushed open the café door. Archer looked left and right, signaling Eddington to follow. Overhead, dark gray clouds covered the sky, but no one had opened their umbrellas. Eddington tucked his head into the collar of his blazer and crossed the street. Over the windy ways, Eddington could see Archer come across a few Prefects, but they didn't stop him. Like black-clothed phantoms, they allowed Archer and Eddington to pass through unhindered. Their expressionless eyes sent a shiver down Eddington's spine.

After a few more crossings, Archer veered into an alley. There were no garbage processing units, but there was a ladder leading up to a fire escape on the right side of the narrow walkway. Archer climbed as Eddington followed, and his nearly healed palms scraped against the flaking black paint. The two arrived on the rooftop outside the scope of the Prefects.

Archer overlooked the streets and, without turning his head, said, "Kid?"

"Yes." Eddington didn't turn his head either.

"It's dangerous. What you did."

"What is?"

"You think I don't know?" Archer turned toward Eddington. "What's under your arm?"

Eddington shifted, keeping his gaze trained on his feet. Muffled sounds of crunching paper revealed his secrets.

"But I had to." Eddington slowly pulled out sheets of paper filled with his scribbles.

"Still the same." Archer chuckled. "All the same."

Eddington smiled too. "Maybe... rebellion wouldn't work. But then..." Eddington turned to Archer. "But what about those... Rogues?"

"They didn't have the wisdom of both worlds." Archer let out a breath. "You still hate The Regime?"

"Not really. It works."

"It works." Archer pulled out a cigarette. His right hand still wasn't steady. "But the Rogues refuse to see that."

"I guess so." Eddington shoved his hands in his pockets.

"But you want something more." Archer turned to him. Eddington stayed quiet. "You want to know." Archer lighted the cigarette. "You want to understand this place."

"I guess so." Eddington shrugged.

"Where are your buds?" Archer turned his eyes back to the streets.

"Here." Eddington reached into his blazer pocket where he had placed the buds a few days before, but they weren't there. "What the..."

"Where?" Archer smiled.

"I think I..." Eddington blushed. "I think I lost them."

"You won't need them anymore." Archer looked at Eddington's hands. "What happened to your hands?"

"Just scratches. They'll be fine. I went to your room, and you weren't there, and... I was chased."

"Never do that. I would've been fine. I'm always fine." Archer dropped the half-smoked cigarette on the ground and ceased the spark with the bottom of his shoe. "We shouldn't be here any longer."

"Goodbye, Archer." He stopped fumbling through his pockets and turned his eyes to the streets below. A few strolling umbrellas passed down on the street; people had begun to distrust the cloudy sky.

Archer walked away, leaving Eddington on the rooftop. With his head still tucked into his gray blazer, Eddington looked over The Regime. He didn't like the place. He didn't *hate* it either.

Chapter 11

Joe was gone.

Ada and Fred sat in chairs in the living room with their arms crossed. A spaced-out look infected their eyes, and they seemed detached. As soon as Eddington entered the hideout, they sat up in their chairs, but their gazes were still absent-minded.

"Where've you been?" Fred didn't look at Eddington.

"I was out."

"Ed, we were—"

"Ada. He…" Fred interrupted.

"What happened?" Eddington shifted his eyes from Fred to Ada. "Where's…"

"Gone." Fred recrossed his arms and sunk a little deeper into the chair.

"When did this—"

"Last night." Fred picked up a half-smoked cigarette from an ashtray on the floor. Ada didn't stop him. "Stupid, stupid, stupid. How did I not see it?" He lit the cigarette again while shaking his head.

"Have you seen him, Ed?" Her large dark eyes glittered on the brink of tears.

"No." He didn't know what to do.

"Where've you been anyway?" Fred stood up from the chair with that cigarette in his hand, taking a step toward Eddington.

"I've been—"

"Yeah, yeah!" He threw the still-burning cigarette onto the floor. The spark of the cigarette scattered into orange pinpricks. "You were out looking for stuff for your own sake! Walking the streets. Are you one of us or not? You and that... whoever. Who are you anyway? Are you actually Eddington? Or are you—" A cough interrupted Fred's frenzy. He raised a fist to his mouth and wheezed out shaky breaths.

Ada went over to him and tapped him on the back. "Fred?"

"I'm fine. I'm fine!" He sat back down with his hands on his knees, his upper body shuddering in time to the erratic rhythm of his breath. "Ed... just who... who are you?"

Eddington stayed put where he stood. "I don't know."

"Ed." Ada rushed over to him and grabbed his arm. "You have to help us find Joe! If you know anything about where he was—"

"That boy's no use to us." Fred covered his eyes with his right hand. His body still rocked back and forth to the rhythm of his breaths. "Bastard's gone. Captured. The guys in black suits followed him and found him. Gone! And that person right there!" He pointed his finger toward Eddington. "He caused it."

"Fred, you can't just—"

"Look at him!" Fred stood with his back straight and struggled for a second to find his balance. "Look at him, Ada. Is anything about him normal? Why wasn't *he* captured? He's with those bastards. Where did you find him anyway?"

"Fred!" Ada was still holding on to Eddington's arm. "He's not one of them."

"How do you know that? Huh? Joe's gone! Who could've caused it, huh?" Another round of coughing racked his thin body. He had to sit back down.

Ada rushed back to Fred, patting him on the back. "Fred, I told you. It won't solve anything. You've gotta stop."

"I'm fine, Ade. Really, I'm fine." Fred turned to Ada, and the two embraced one another in a hug.

Eddington stood speechless. Joe was gone. Probably forever. Like a heartless monster, The Regime engulfed him, never to spit him out again. Joe was just another Rogue squashed by the boot of the Regime.

"Fred, I'm sorry." Eddington's eyes softened.

"No, you're not," Fred uttered as he pointed toward the door of the hideout. "Get out!"

"Ed!" Ada's voice broke, and she reached out her arm. "Ed?"

"Maybe it's for the best." Eddington took a sharp turn into his room. He snatched all the pages he had scribbled on and hid them beneath his blazer.

"Ed!" Ada stopped him at the door of his room. "I—"

"What?"

"I don't…" Teardrops came rolling down her left cheek.

"Look, I said it's for the best." Eddington straightened up his lapel.

"You have to be safe. Promise me." More tears rolled down her cheeks. "I'll see you at L'Académie?"

"Maybe. I have to go."

"Ada?" Fred called from the living room. Eddington's eyes were dry.

"But—"

"Ada." Eddington neared and kissed her gently on the forehead. "Goodbye." He walked toward the living room and saw Fred staring at the bookshelf. "Fred…"

"Just go." He had his back turned. Cigarette fume surrounded him as two coughs shook his body.

Eddington turned away and trudged up the stairs. The stairs creaked with each step he took. Upon reaching the exit door, he took one last glance into the hideout. Ada was at the bottom of the stairwell. She looked at him with watery eyes.

Chapter 12

Who the hell was he anyway? Fred had asked him so many times, but Eddington had no answer. What was wrong with him? He didn't have any clue about who he was. He didn't know why his father smiled at the tree. He didn't know where they took his father after the arrest. He couldn't even remember his father's face. The man was just—gone. Like Joe. Forever. That was certain.

Eddington walked along the street with pages hidden under his blazer. Prefects no longer bothered him—not even for his missing earbuds. He passed by the café window. Through it, he saw Tom, and they waved at one another with bright smiles.

Back at his apartment, nothing much had changed in the two weeks he'd been gone. The same militant men guarded The Wall; the sun slanted through the window just as it had before; his room as still ordered and bare. But something was different. The room's system kicked into gear, and the speaker spoke: "Sir, how are you today?"

"I've been out." He took off his blazer and threw it on the couch.

"Sir, your meal proportions are unbalanced."

"Thank you."

"Standard portion?"

"Make it a double, thanks."

The machine on the living room stool rumbled. Two silver packets rolled out. Eddington grabbed them and tore open the packages.

I am digesting dully at the stove...

He recalled.

I hate those Prefects.

Not really.

He ate the meal out of the packets and went to the bathtub where the cameras wouldn't see him. The triple screen, along with the lighting system, turned themselves off. Eddington pulled the pages out from his blazer and continued to write with his short, stubby pencil. The light through the shutters of the bathroom dimmed as the stripes of slim rectangles on the tiled floor disappeared. It was a relief. Though it was a crime to do so, it was also the only way to recover his sanity and preserve his mind. Eddington paused and accustomed his eyes to the dark room. Where did all the books go? How did The Regime come about? Where was she now?

Where was she now?

Eddington looked at the sentence he had just scribbled down. He took a deep breath and stood up in the bathtub. The system turned itself back on. He needed to find Archer again.

***

He continued to go back to L'Académie. The signal was disrupted, though at times, he wished it wasn't. Sometimes, he saw Ada wandering around The Square after her sessions, but they never acknowledged one another. Day by day, he began to forget the details of her face.

He went back to the café to talk to Tom. Each day, that guy seemed to grow more knowledgeable. Eddington no longer answered any of his quizzes about historical facts, for he didn't know many of the things he mentioned.

He continued to scribble in the bathtub. The same routine—the darkened house, the pen against the page—settled him to his own thoughts. The more he wrote, the more agitated he grew. Questions, questions, questions. Where were the books? The girl? His dad?

***

"Ever seen one of these?" Archer turned to Eddington.

"Not recently."

Archer and Eddington were sitting on the edge of an old abandoned building as Archer waved a hardcover book in front of him.

"When was the last time?"

"When I was with… some Rogues."

"Ah. Right." Archer set the book down.

"Archer?" Eddington slowly moved toward Archer and looked at the cover. "Why are these things banned?"

"L'Académie…" Archer took a deep breath. "It wasn't really a ban."

"How so?"

"People stopped reading. A long time ago, anyway."

"Right. *General will…*" Those words weren't his own.

"Oh?" Archer turned to look at Eddington. "Impressive."

"Not really, never read the whole thing. Read it from some French Revolution book."

"You know what this one is?" Archer held up the hardcover again.

It looked strangely familiar to Eddington's eyes. The stream, the girl, the untouched door...

"Flip it open."

Eddington took the book from Archer. The texture of the cover brought him back to that tree stump. He could almost smell the damp grass under his feet. The weighty block of text brought back a string of faint images. *The trickling stream. The girl.* He flipped open to a random page, and those images, once faint, cleared up.

Walk with me...

"Where did you get this?" Eddington looked at Archer.

"I have my ways." Archer reached for a cigarette from his pocket only to find an empty compartment. "Damn it."

"That won't solve things." Eddington shrugged and almost smiled.

"I'll try." Archer smiled at Eddington. For a second, Eddington thought he'd seen it somewhere before.

"But then…" Eddington turned his head, overlooking the streets of The Regime. "Where are the rest of these… books?"

"Where do you think?" Archer was still looking for a cigarette.

"They burned them?"

"That's stupid." Archer gave a dry cough.

Eddington paused to think. "Why did they take them?"

"Kid, quiet." Suddenly, Archer moved away from the edge of the building, pulling Eddington down with him. The two ducked away from sight, and Archer peeked his head up over the edge of the building. Archer tapped Eddington on the shoulder. "Look."

Below, there was a band of Prefects. A gray truck was humming down the vacant streets. Volumes upon volumes of books teetered on the back of the truck.

"What the…"

"Shhh!" Archer pointed at the truck. "Watch."

A group in dark suits held crates in their hands. The colorful covers were dumped into the back of the humming gray truck. Once the dark suits emptied all their crates at hand, they climbed onto the sides of the slow-moving truck.

"Garbage season," Archer muttered.

"Where are they going?"

"Shh, keep watching."

The gray truck accelerated. Before, it was like a mother duck, patiently strolling along the streets, waiting for those little specks of men in black suits to catch up. But as all the men in black suits climbed and grabbed onto the side rails, the humming beast took off into the distance. It went so fast Eddington feared that sudden movements—either from a strong gust of winter wind or some random bump along the road— would knock off a few of those dark specks.

"I need to... know where it goes." Eddington rolled up his blazer's sleeves.

"Kid, you can try." Archer was still rummaging through his empty pockets. "You ain't gonna catch up with it."

"Where are they going?" He clenched his fists, squatting down next to Archer and holding his gaze. "What are they gonna do with them?"

Archer still rummaged through his empty pockets. "I need to go."

"Tell me."

"Kid, there'll be another time." He strolled toward the fire escape with hurried steps. Eddington watched the man with the long dark coat climb down the ladder.

For a split second, he smiled at Eddington. That was it—Eddington did know that smile.

The humming gray truck was far gone into the windy streets. The array of books was scattered in the back of the truck like litter on the street.

Garbage season.

Chapter 13

Eddington stood in front of the store, leaning against a white pipe. People passed him by, going about their business like every other day. It was the strangest thing. Normality was no longer normal. The Regime ran like clockwork, but little instances reminded Eddington that the people in it were people after all. The moments were brief and inconsistent—like people. On The Box one day, a younger boy turned and met his gaze, then quickly looked away. It was just one moment of eye contact in a sea of people staring down, but still. Then, on the way toward the café, he saw the young couple again. They sat closer to one another. Even when Eddington passed by, they still held on to each other's hands.

He entered the café and ordered a cup of hot chocolate at the counter. His favorite seat was unoccupied, so he plopped down to enjoy his drink. Before, he'd never paid any real attention to the other patrons at the café. But he'd become more intrigued and began to notice little details that were out of the ordinary. A man stared at his screen as he tapped his feet to a rhythm only he could hear—as if some private symphony played in his head. Subtle movements of solitary delight showed in his bright eyes and the gentle swaying of his body. A girl in a navy blazer looked down at her screen, but from time to time, her gaze wandered to the streets outside the café.

In the grand orchestra of The Regime, there was a musical unity. The inconsistencies—they were human. Yet viewed as a whole, The Regime swept irregularities away. The place still ran like clockwork. Students could never escape the thoughts imbedded by L'Académie.

Eddington sat with his paper cup, lost in thought. The door of the café swung open, and in came the Man of History.

"Hey, Tom." Eddington lifted his cup.

"Oh, surprise, surprise." Tom greeted Eddington as he headed toward the counter to get a cup.

"How do you do?"

"Not too bad." Tom tapped on the screen and selected his beverage. "Saw the truck running down earlier."

"The truck?"

"Yeah. Haven't you seen it around?"

"Where did you see it?"

"Just on my way here. You know, crossing the stop at The Box and down the left street. It just ran past me. Didn't even get a chance to see what was on it. Too fast, you know."

The machine on the counter beeped. The drink was ready.

"Do you know where it was going?"

"Nah." Tom took a sip of his drink from the paper cup. "It went by, and just like that, gone!"

"You know what's on the back of that truck, right?"

"What?" Tom made his way back to the sitting area.

"Books."

"Books?" Tom's gaze widened as his frame jolted and a few drops of hot coffee landed on the ground. "You mean actual books?"

"Yeah."

"Never seen one. Really? Books? Hmm." Tom nodded his head while pacing around the café.

"Wait, wait, wait." The man who'd been tapping his feet came over to Tom and Eddington. "Those things are still around?"

"According to him," Tom replied as he tilted his head toward Eddington.

"You know those things are prohibited, right?" the foot tapper asked.

"I know. But why are they?"

"Why? Did you say *why*?" The foot tapper widened his eyes. "I'll have you know it's a *prohibited item*," he uttered, his chin raised with a sour look.

"It's fine. He didn't mean it." Tom placed his hand on Eddington's shoulder. When their eyes met, Eddington saw a flash of inconsistency in Tom's gaze—something that had never been there before. It was the echo of a human quality in the Man of History—no, in Tom. He took a seat on the couch opposite Eddington.

"Friend," he said to the foot tapper. "Your name?"

"Max. History branch?"

"Yes, yes." The Man of History smiled. "You?"

"Chemical Engineering."

"I should've known! Your blazer's color!"

Eddington sat; the same agitation made its return, and it made him sick to his stomach. The Man of History was back, and Tom was gone. The man named Max sat with them, making them a company of three, though only two participated in the chatter.

Pure orthodoxies!

Eddington scribbled on the page. He was back in his bathtub. On his right, a few books were stacked in a tower on the verge of falling. On his left, crumpled pages filled with pencil marks littered the floor.

After a few hours, Eddington tucked the pages away. The minute he took a step out of the tub, the lighting system of the apartment complex jumped back to life. The three-paneled living room screen was back on. He made his way to the couch and took a seat, eyes tired and adrift. The speaker aired: "Sir, what would you—"

"No, thank you. Go dark." The speaker didn't respond. LED lights turned off as the living room was once again plunged into darkness. The only source of light came from the bathroom, which couldn't be turned off when he was in the house.

He lay down as his brain raced through an avalanche of thoughts. They toyed with his mind and kept him awake, and he tossed and turned with every new worry.

The light began to distort and fade. The single bathroom door slowly blurred into two white rectangles. He jolted back awake with a sharp breath, and the light came into focus. But moments later, the rectangle began to split again. His eyelids grew heavier. He took another breath, and the bathroom light darkened.

Chapter 14

The young man stood on the side of the street. A bag was slung across his shoulder, and he held a book wrapped in blue paper.

He was heading toward the bakery, but he wasn't all that interested in the bread. As he walked among the streets, the chilling wind brushed against him, but it was a soft caress, not a vicious shove. The more he walked, the warmer he got, and eventually, he forgot about the cold wind altogether.

She'd begun working at the bakery ever since her parents left. During one of their walks, she'd explained what happened. One day, she said, some of the same men they'd seen in the forest showed up at the door and told her parents about a special work placement. She never saw them again.

More and more people were assigned to the placement. Like his mother. For the first few weeks, she seemed like the same mom he'd always known. The only difference was the addition of the blazer. But then she started acting strange, and eventually, she was sent away. But at least she seemed to have a choice. His father was arrested. It all happened so fast. The young man was in his room, looking out of the window to the street. His father was there, close to a tree, and he looked up, and they locked eyes. His face was full of complexities, of love and fear and hope and hopelessness. Within seconds, the expression turned into a smile—but not directed to his son. To the tree. His smile morphed to loud laughter, then muffled laughter as the black-suited men shoved a cloth bag over his head. And just like that, his father was gone.

Throughout the days following his father's arrest, libraries were emptied as trucks hurled through the streets, carrying volumes of books. The last survivors were bookshops. The day before, as the young man bought a book wrapped in blue wrapping paper, the red-headed shop manager told him he was buying the last of the remaining books. Stock wasn't coming. The shop would probably close down.

He stood at the traffic light. Before, the car lanes were a mess of chaos and honking as people drove home. But ever since the black-suited men arrived, traffic looked strangely uniform. The pedestrian light turned green; the young man hurried off in a straight line toward the bakery where she worked.

A trace of nervousness overcame him as he smelled freshly baked bread outside the bakery. He tried to calm himself, focusing on the breeze blowing past as he huddled in his winter coat and scarf, but he still behaved like a little kid in a candy shop. He lingered in front of the bakery; someone in a navy blazer walked past him. On the opposite side of the street, there was a man in a black suit. The young man lingered for a few more moments, then eased himself into the bakery. It warmed him immediately, the smell of sweet pastries and hot coffee welcoming him in.

She was there, but she didn't notice him at first. She was lost in her work. Her hair was tied up as she shuffled along those aisles of freshly baked bread. All of her focus was on blocks of grain set to be rearranged and sliced pieces to be packaged. Morning customers waited patiently in a line as they stared down at the glowing displays of delicious sweets.

The young man was at the back of the line. He held tight to the book wrapped in blue paper. It was a gift, a surprise of sorts, that he wished to give her right after she finished work.

The line moved. One by one, customers grabbed hold of their share of grain and left the warmth of the bakery. The young man moved closer and closer to the counter.

Out came a tall blond boy. "Good morning, sir. What can I get you?"

The young man quickly tucked away the gift in his hands and pretended to browse the assortments in the glass display. For a split second, he glanced at her. She was still lost in arranging the blocks of grain and packaging the slices of bread.

"I will have a croissant, please."

"Sure thing, sir. That's three dollars."

"Thank you."

A black-suited man passed by the bakery, and everyone stopped. The clerk's right hand hovered in midair just as he reached to pick up the young man's croissant. The woman cleaning was wide-eyed as she froze in place, bending to pick up a wrapper. The girl behind the counter rested her hands on freshly baked grain, her head turned slightly toward the black-suited man. The young man stood still; the wrapped book clutched tightly in his arms. Dead silence fell over the café; a heater hummed in the background.

The black-suited man adjusted his spectacles and slowly walked up to the young man. His uptight manners gave him chills, even in the heated room.

"Sir, you're carrying a prohibited item."

"But I just got it yesterday."

"Sir, it's prohibited."

"But..." The young man turned his head and met the gaze of the girl. Her eyes brightened in the midst of the tense exchange, but there was a guarded air about her as the black-suited man loomed over them.

"Sir, I shall have that."

"But..." The young man looked over to the girl once more. She nodded and smiled at him.

"Sir?"

"Fine, you can have it."

"Thank you." The black-suited man took the book wrapped in blue paper and parted from the bakery. Everything returned to normal. The clerk checked out the croissant, and the lady continued mopping the floor, though her eyes were on the young man.

"Here it is. You have a great day, sir." The tall blond boy handed over the croissant in a brown paper bag.

"Yes, thank you." The young man grabbed the bag and was about to leave the bakery. After just a few steps away from the counter, he heard someone running up to him. A few more steps, and her arms were around him again.

"Thank you," the girl whispered into his ear. She quickly pulled herself back and returned to the isles of bread. The young man smiled and left the bakery.

He was back outside, taking a few deep breaths as he tried to make sense of what had happened. Several men in black suits roamed the streets—including the one who took the book. Eddington followed him down a few blocks, trying to be as furtive as he could, but the man knew he was being followed. A few times, he glanced back. At a crosswalk, he stopped and leveled his gaze at the young man, who jolted and turned down another street, eager to get away.

As he continued walking, he saw a bearded man sitting on the curb. He was so covered in filth that Eddington didn't register him at first.

"Y'all ain't get none!" the man on the corner muttered to himself as he shook his head. He was wearing a torn sweater, and an old shoe dangled from his right hand. Wild blue eyes latched on to the young man's.

"Sorry?"

"Ain't no one pays them attention. Look'ee them!" The strange man banged the old shoe against the pavement.

"Who?"

"Them Pre-facts!" The banging of the shoe became more rapid.

"Joe?"

"Ya monster, Ed. Wasn't I good enough to you? Ya sniffling rat." The banging of the shoe grew louder.

"Joe, I'm—"

"Sorry?"

"Joe…"

Another deep, sharp breath. Eddington woke up from the couch with a numb right leg. Someone was knocking on the door. He hopped toward the door and opened it.

"Good afternoon, how can I…"

"Sir." There was a band of Prefects at his door. Two of them were holding onto Ada's arms. She struggled against the grip, but the effort was fruitless. "We'd like to ask you a few questions."

Eddington stood there and breathed deeply. "Yes?"

"By any chance, sir, do you know this girl?" The inquiring Prefect turned to Ada.

"What are you going to do to her?"

"Sir, this isn't the question. Do you know her and her conduct?"

"I don't know what you're getting at."

Another Prefect at the back reached into his pocket and handed something to the leader.

"Do you know what these are?"

They were the chips that disrupted the signal on the terminals. Eddington's right hand started to tremble. The Prefects didn't notice it.

"No."

"Then do you associate with her in any way?" The speaking Prefect looked over at Ada again. There was a brief, nauseating silence where a decision dangled in the air. Ada looked at Eddington with dark eyes that glittered with just a spark of hope.

"No."

His heart wrenched as he saw the spark in Ada's eyes flicker and die. Her rebellion and savviness melted away. She became an ant waiting to be squashed by a bored child. Once, she might've thought she was the hero of her story. And maybe sometimes that was Fred or Joe. But that had crumbled—all because of a word. A word he'd said.

"Thank you, sir." The speaking Prefect took a step closer to Eddington and peeked into his unit. "Is everything all right in there?"

"Ah, yes. Yes."

"The system is blinking on and off. Do you need a checkup?"

"No, it's okay."

"Then"—the Prefect took a step back—"good day to you, sir."

"Wait. Why are you taking her?" He took a step toward the Prefects.

"You spoke a prohibited item. That's your first warning. Good day." The Prefect turned his back and, with the rest of the band, carried Ada away. Ada shuffled forward, not a trace of rebellion left in her eyes. She complied so willingly to the Prefects it was as if all of her life and convictions wilted away in the span of a few minutes. Eddington watched her march as he stood in the doorway, telling himself he couldn't have done anything differently. Not if he wanted to live.

Chapter 15

"Archer?" Eddington had his hands in his pockets, and his neck was tucked against the cold. "Where do they take people who've been arrested?" Five days had passed since Ada was taken away, and Eddington still didn't know what had happened to her.

"Well." Archer was sitting on top of a garbage processing unit. "They disappear."

"Forever?"

"I believe they go through a reform program. Similar to L'Académie, but more targeted."

"Targeted to what?"

"I don't know." Archer's face twitched a bit.

"But..." Eddington hesitated before asking the question. "Why haven't the Prefects arrested you?"

"I play by their rules." Archer smiled.

"No, you don't."

"I pretend to." He jumped off the garbage processing unit.

"But how come others are arrested for small crimes, and you're able to get away with so much? And... I was able to..." Eddington paused.

"Yes?" Archer leaned toward Eddington, his eyebrows raised with a smile still pasted on his face.

Something finally clicked. He felt uneasy. His behavior could never have passed the watchful eyes of the Prefects. If they wanted to arrest him, they would've done it a long time ago.

"The point is, how did I get away with so much?" Eddington looked at Archer.

"You hide things quite well." He shrugged.

"But Ada is..."

"Hmm?"

A brief silence. A gust of wind blew through the alleyway.

"Who's Ada?"

"No one."

Archer raised his brows. "The one who got arrested?"

"Yeah."

"Very well." Archer rested his hand on his shoulder. "Very well."

Eddington glanced at the hand on his shoulder in confusion. He couldn't make sense of what Archer meant. A Prefect passed by. He looked at Archer and Eddington for a brief moment and continued walking.

"Well, what?" Eddington brushed Archer's hand away.

"You'll see." Archer nodded. "I know you have a lot of questions. But there's one thing you can be sure of. You are not one of them. Don't pretend you are."

"Sorry?" He took a step back from Archer.

"You're right. If those bastards wanted to arrest us, they would've done it a long time ago. I don't think The Regime is kind."

"No…"

Archer sighed as he rubbed his forehead. He stopped and held Eddington's gaze. "You want to know where the books went?"

Eddington nodded.

"It's about time I tell you this. Those trucks, Ed. They carry the books off to The Archive. It's a kind of vault where they keep all the original texts. Then The Plant digitizes and distributes all of it to L'Académie."

A sudden flash of insight. Eddington recalled those scenes from his distant dream: the metal rim, the capsule, the forest.

"Your mother, you told me, works at The Plant. Everyone trained in the Humanities works there. Those who are trained for more scientific disciplines either work as Engineers at The Corner or as Researchers."

"Are the research institutions beyond The Wall?"

"What do you think?"

"But…"

"But what?"

"Why don't they just teach the original books?"

Archer laughed and almost choked on the cigarette smoke.

"No one *wants* to do that. They want to take the easy way. Reading, Ed—would it be crazy to say reading is hard? We're way past that. Rapid information ingestion became the norm; depth became irrelevant. If you can learn just by sitting there for two hours with no effort, who wouldn't take that?"

"Then… does that mean…" Eddington scratched his head.

"People don't think anyway." Archer exhaled. "Original works are too dangerous. You remember The Cross? How it drives people mad?"

"Yes."

"Sanity is consensus."

Sanity is consensus.

Eddington was in the bathtub with a short stubby pencil, scribbling away in the dark. Besides him lay a few books without titles—no markers hinted at their origins, but that made them even more intriguing.

He was no longer afraid because of what Archer had told him. He was special. The Prefects never had any intention of arresting him. But Eddington couldn't fully trust that; he still hid his books in the bathtub and avoided the cameras in his apartment.

The racing tip of the pencil still supplied him with a string of pleasure. While he wrote, he revealed a part of himself he'd never discovered. Writing was his salvation. It was his escape. He needed those moments to remove himself from the madness outside. There was no way he could count on himself to keep the mess at bay. Only Archer could help him make sense of everything going on.

He'd stopped attending L'Académie sessions since the Prefects had removed the disruptors from the terminals. There was no need for him to go back anyway. No one really cared. No one expected him. In a sense, he was free. In another sense, he was neglected—no one really cared.

"Now, you see." Archer had held up a copy of another book without a cover. "These things are not meant to be read that easily."

"It made my skin crawl…" Eddington shook his head. "The duel at the end was… vivid and just… why did he…"

"You think those from L'Académie could handle this?"

Against the dim light from the window, Eddington's focus returned back to the bathtub and the book in his hands. Those vivid characters stirred and sunk his heart at different points of the plot. But hours after straining his eyes, they merely glided over the ink. His mind had slipped elsewhere. He had lost track of time, and his eyes blurred so much he couldn't read another page. The lighting system turned back on as he got out of the bathtub. On his way out the door, he grabbed hold of his gray blazer; the wind had been chilly and unforgiving all day. One step after another; the street was but passing visions. The guards policing The Wall appeared to him comical characters, standing ground for their just duties. As people strolled by, Eddington wondered about their backstories. How did they end up at L'Académie? Why did they consign themselves to a life so dull? He stumbled his way along the street, veering from left to right, bumping into a few passersby. His reading obscured the orderliness and smudged the sharp edges of regulations in The Regime.

He noticed more of those human traits. On the corner of the street, the young couple held hands on the curb; the girl rested her head on the boy's shoulder. He averted his eyes and made a turn toward the café. On his way, he saw a rolling coffee cup out on the street. He picked it up, looked at it, and dropped it again. A warm cup was what he needed.

"You! Sir!"

"Hey, Tom." He made his way over to where the man always sat.

"Now, tell me. That thing. Napoleon Bonaparte."

"Hmmm."

"Come on. Where's that wit you had?"

He had a quote in his head from another book, but he didn't want to say it aloud. Tom might freak out.

"Maybe I'm not as sharp as I was before." He shrugged.

"Haven't seen you around The Square much. What happened? What happened to that girl? Haven't seen her either."

"Gone."

"Really? Beyond The Wall?"

"Not quite." Remorse still coursed through him as he remembered the arrest of Ada and Joe. It was a cruel, cruel place. People disappeared in the blink of an eye.

The Regime had them controlled and conquered. Eddington sympathized with them, but there was another part of himself that saw no point in shedding tears for fugitives.

"So where?"

"Tom, no more questions. You're approaching a prohibited limit."

Tom looked at him.

Something was different. Eddington paused. "Did The Cross happen to you?"

"No." He pointed at his buds. "Working perfectly fine."

"See any Double-Rods recently?"

"No."

"Very well." Eddington turned around and paused at the door. He nodded once, pushed the handle, and was back out on the streets. Cars passed by, reminding him of the old carriages of a place called London— he'd read about them in his books. People walked along the streets, and he chuckled at their boring ways. They knew so little and yet were content to continue. He wasn't like them. He observed. He noticed. Like the bare branches of winter, so picturesque and nostalgic that they brought a smile to his face. But his soothing moment did not last; a dark-suited man appeared behind him.

"Sir. No stopping on the streets," a Prefect said.

"Sorry." He kept walking. The Prefect paid him no mind, continuing his patrol of the streets.

He took a left turn onto an empty street. His steps, once heavy and rhythmic, began to feel light as if the soles of his shoes were no longer glued to the ground. He began hopping. The streets were empty; no one was around to witness his happy madness. He hid himself away in an alley and danced to the tunes of his inner symphony. His lightened steps turned into some grand, expressive theatre; his moves needed no audience. Happiness washed over him, perhaps for the first time.

He settled after a while of dancing around. He knew for sure if he kept going, he too would be put away. The Regime could not tolerate a happy man spiraling into madness in a random backstreet. He sat down next to a garbage processing unit at the back of the alley, pulled out his dull pencil and yellow page, and began scribbling. Amidst the humming noise came a snap. The graphite tip broke and slowly rolled onto the pavement. Eddington looked at the rolling tip and realized he was sitting under someone's shadow.

In the midst of the hum, he heard a voice say, "Still writing?" It came from above. "You still writing?" Whoever it was raised his voice.

Eddington raised his head as fear mingled with remorse trembled his right hand. The pencil without a graphite tip fell out of his hand and clattered against the concrete. Eddington's gaze stayed fixed on the man squatting atop the garbage unit above him.

"I asked you, boy, are you still writing?"

"Fred, look, I..." Eddington was frozen in place. The threat of being shot could do that to a person— Fred had a gun.

"You did this." Fred pointed the gun. "You piece of shit."

"Fred!" Eddington's hands were in the air. "I'm sorry, but..."

"Nothing to be sorry about. Where's Ada?" Fred shook his gun.

"She..."

"Where is she? First there was Joe, and then Ada. Now it has to be you! Has to be you!"

"Fred, it's not what you—"

"Shut up! Shut up." The man, once calm, began to sob. He wiped his tears with his sleeves. Eddington slowly got up from the corner as Fred wiped his tears, but Fred immediately pointed the gun back at him.

"You. Don't you *dare* go." The sobs continued.

"What you're doing here is dangerous."

"How? The Prefects? Tell you what, I don't fear. They will... di-die, I... will... will shoot them if the... they try to save you."

"Fred." Eddington looked up at a surveillance camera. "They know what you're doing here."

"I... don't give a..." The sobbing slowly quieted. "Just who are you anyway? Are you with them? Tell me!" Fred jumped down from the unit and stalked closer and closer to Eddington. The cold gun's tip almost touched Eddington's forehead. "Who are you?"

Eddington could see tears rolling down that stubbled face. "I don't know."

"Enough!"

A heavy blow hit his left temple; he'd never imagined getting shot would be that painless. His thoughts muddled, and he slipped away to a peaceful sleep.

Chapter 16

"Did you see her this morning?" he asked, running up to the counter despite the long line of waiting customers.

"No. She's supposed to be here, though." The tall blond boy whipped out a piece of paper. "The roster says she was supposed to be here a few hours ago."

"When was... the last time... you saw her?" He paused, gulping down air as he tried to catch his breath.

"She was here two days ago for her shift." The tall boy slid his finger along the sheet. "Eleven hundred hours to sixteen hundred hours, it says here."

"Right." The young man's head dropped, his hands still atop the display. "Damn it, damn it, damn it."

"Is everything all right, sir?" The tall boy put the roster sheet down.

He lifted his head and forced a smile. Two palm marks remained on top of the glass cabinet as he made his way out of the bakery.

"It can't be..." muttered the young man as he walked down the street. "It can't... it can't be... she doesn't even…" He stopped in his tracks as a band of students in navy blazers walked past him. Laughter floated down the street as they bantered back and forth, enjoying the bright day and company of friends. But as soon as a black suit appeared on the opposite side of the street, the joy stopped. It was as if a switch was flipped; the students walked with their backs erect, marching in a straight line down the street.

He watched the suited students for a bit before continuing down the street. "There's no…" As he walked, he focused on his feet, ridden with confused thoughts. "Where is…" In the midst of his thoughts, he jumped back as he collided with someone. He looked up and stared into an empty gaze.

"Sir." It was the man in a black suit.

"Sorry. I'm really sorry."

"By any means, are you in the program yet?"

"Which is…" He looked up at him with his back hunched.

"It is mandatory, judging by your age." The dark suit pulled out a portable rectangular screen from his pocket. "Your profile fits that of…" The black suit frowned as he looked at the screen. "You are…"

"Yes?"

"Never mind, sir. You are free to go." The black-suited man slipped the screen back into his pocket and strolled off.

"Thank you." The young man stood still where he was. What was the program he talked about? He must have been muttering to himself—people gave him strange looks as they passed. He shook himself awake and continued walking down the street.

The movements of people among the streets, which were so disorderly and human just moments before, were flattened into a monotony of order. Some people still did not wear the newly issued blazers, but they were few and far between.

None of the people who passed by noticed him. They were indifferent to everyone else on the street. The young man stopped again, that time not from the fear of encountering another black-suited man but from a speck of familiarity in the midst of the roiling crowd. It startled him. His senses zeroed in on that one figure amongst the indifferent many. He saw the familiar outline of a young woman. Her back was to him as she strolled away, but he'd recognize her anywhere. She was still in a white sleeveless dress, even in the cold wind. Her hair whirled, its disorder stark against the backdrop of the monotonous crowd. The young man struggled through the current of people like a salmon swimming upstream as he fought his way to her. As he pushed his way through the crowd, their grunts all sounded the same, like they were computer-generated instead of human sounds. The young woman was drifting farther away, almost swallowed up by the blazers. He forced his way through the stream of people, his eyes set on her blonde hair. In a fit of desperation, the young man yelled: "Amelia!"

All those walking figures in blazers stopped their steps. They fixed their vacant eyes on the young man's agitated face. The only one who kept walking was Amelia, her steps graceful and light. As she walked, the crowd of blazers parted for her like she was a beacon of light cutting through dark storm clouds. She moved farther and farther away.

"Amelia!"

The plea didn't slow her down a bit. Her steps lightened and became little hops along the ground. The dark crowd, distancing themselves from Amelia, left her enough room to hop and dance farther and farther away.

"Please! Amelia!"

The crowd still followed the young man's movements. They formed a uniform tide against him, working together to push him back. It was a dark gush of flowing blazers determined to wash him away, forcing a wide chasm between the lovers. In the distance, the girl in the white dress skipped away.

"Amelia!"

A harsh gush of wind whirled and whistled. The shrill noise amplified like a whip cutting through the air.

Snap!

A sharp crackle of pain crossed Eddington's chest, leaving a burning sensation that ripped Eddington out of his dream. The dark crowd disappeared. The girl in the sleeveless white dress was gone. The visions were replaced by sensations of a crude rope rubbing against his wrists and the residue of pain on his chest. He was tied up. His hands were behind him, and he was unable to move.

"Amelia, eh?" Fred held a belt, lightly tapping it against his left hand as if he were practicing for the next blow. A yellow tungsten bulb flickering on the ceiling provided the only light in the room. It illuminated his face, showing the yellow sheen of his skin and his hair sticking up in tufts.

Eddington glanced around, recognizing the hideout. It had one been homey and welcoming, but those qualities, like Ada and Joe, were gone. Dust covered every surface, and a rancid smell hung in the dead air. Clothing was scattered across the couch. Crumpled-up pages torn from books decorated the room, and broken pieces of plates were sprinkled on the floor.

"Whey, hey-hey! Where'you looking, buddy?" Fred cracked the belt on a bench next to him. "You think they'll save you here?"

"Fred, I'm not working with them."

"Bullshit!" The belt traveled from left of his cheek to the root of his neck and made a crisp sound. "How then? Huh? They took you in; Ada took you in. And then they were arrested? Too perfect of a narrative, is it not?"

"What... do you... want, Fred?"

"I want them back!"

"I... can't help... help you. I don't even... know where they..."

Another whip across the right cheek and neck, missing his eye by an inch. The whipped area on Eddington's face turned pale for a second, then turned an angry red color.

"I want them back!"

Eddington could feel the start of the tremor in his right hand. Another blow cracked down right after, across his chest that time.

"Are you listening?"

"Fred... I don't know where..."

Another crack.

"Who are you?"

"I... don't..."

Fred punched Eddington in the face, swaying him to his side. It took a little for him to sit back up.

"*Why?* Damn it! Why are you at L'Académie?" Eddington could hear Fred's teeth grind through the shouted words, terrified as the red face drew closer to his own.

"I..."

Fred kicked him on the ribcage. The chair—with Eddington still tied to it—crashed to the ground.

"Tell me how you learned to write!"

The blows rained down, first against Eddington's left arm, then against his ribs, then against his neck. His left ear rang.

"Who's that old man, Ed?" Through the ringing, Eddington could only make out "old man."

"Old... old man..." Eddington twisted in a pool of pain despite the pull of the ropes across his body.

"Huh?" Fred laid down the belt for a second and knelt down. "Old man?"

"I... I don't know..."

"Hmm." Fred slowly climbed to his feet. He helped Eddington up and patted him on the head. "Good. Good. Shhhh." Fred closed his eyes. "Shhh. I'm sorry—I'm so sorry." He made his way to the bench and pulled out a pair of pliers. "Maybe this will force some sense out of you."

Screams of pain escaped from the closed doors of the hideout, but they traveled no farther than the alleyway. People strolling on the streets remained blissfully unaware of what was happening behind the closed doors, thinking of their screens and L'Académie and their meal packets. They weren't worried. Flakes of white drifted among the dull gray buildings, blanketing the hum of the world. A few people looked up for mere moments, only to return to the trudge of the herd. The rest hurried along, dusting the snow off their blazers.

"Now you talk."

Blood dripped from Eddington's left hand onto the ground behind the chair. The tungsten bulb buzzed and flashed; his fingernail lay in a pool of blood.

"Fred… that's all I… know…" Clenching his teeth, Eddington fought to stay conscious, his right hand under sporadic spasms.

"All you told me was his name! Archer?"

"Yes…"

Fred regained the belt, and another whip slashed across his chest.

"He's with the regime!"

"No… he's not…"

"You mean that one in the long coat? He *is*!"

Another blow, softer that time. Fred wheezed, choked breaths oozing out as he struggled for air. "He… is…"

Eddington had no more strength to argue. His chin drooped against his chest, the pain too great to do anything other than look at the floor. For a while, Fred didn't speak to him; he was probably out for a smoke. Blood kept dripping from his hand to the floor, and his world spun. *He's with The Regime… He's with The Regime…* Flashbacks came to him as Eddington recalled those subtle nods and smiles as he told Archer about Ada's arrest. *The Regime isn't kind… You're different from the rest…* Archer's voice echoed. At that instant, something clicked in Eddington's mind. His heart raced, and he gasped for air. He lifted his head with the little strength he had left.

I am with The Regime.

"You know." Fred was back with a cigarette in hand. He looked a lot more relaxed. "I want to kill you, I really do. But I need you for now, Ed. Consider it an old friend's favor."

Fred dragged the chair with Eddington in it, leaving a dotted path of red.

"Oh, here." With the tender care of a loving parent, Fred took out white bandages and wrapped them around Eddington's bleeding finger. "That should do."

His entire body ached. He was a ragdoll, dwindling with the motions dictated by Fred. There was no will nor strength to fight the man. Moments later, Fred dragged Eddington back into his old room and left him there.

"Now, stay here!" The door slammed shut.

Chapter 17

The young man went out the garden's back gate. He trailed through the woods with the only book he had left. The streets had changed, he thought. The whole world had. Before, there was so much chaos, but that was kind of the way of it all. Good or bad, helpful or hurtful, the world was always a jumble of random events. But as more and more people began to wear blazers, everything was just too—predictable. Orderly. Strange. Occasionally, official officers would knock on his door with their bloated bellies and funny-looking ties, pitching some government program for alternative education. He declined all those offers, but he knew it wouldn't be long until he was left with no choice.

He drifted through the woods in a dark mood; it had been four weeks since he'd last seen her. Many of the little details that used to amuse and lighten his heart were poisoned by her disappearance. Everything looked dull, as if the life was drained from the forest once she was gone. The little stump where she once sat, where he held her hand and she traced the lines on his palm, stood alone against the chilly air. With his lover taken and his father arrested, he was like the stump— lonely and broken.

That was his best guess. The black suits had taken her, funneling her into their alternative program. He'd never see her again.

He took out his book and began to read. Every line, every rhyme and step through the plot reminded him of her.

"You should be a poet."

Her soft arms around his skinny frame. Her head on his shoulders. Her hands pressed gently against his.

"Read it to me."

Her bare feet, depressing the patches of grass. Rays of sunshine through her beautiful blonde hair.

"Sir, you're carrying a prohibited item."

They took away everything. They took away his father. They took away his mother. They took away Amelia. He hated them.

The young man closed his book and kept on trailing through the woods. In the distance, he could see a capsule embedded into the ground. At the moment, four black suits guarded it, their sharp eyes scanning the woods. The young man slipped behind a tree, hopeful they hadn't noticed him. He examined the capsule, wondering what it was for. A humming sound roared from the opposite side of the clearing, and a gray truck rumbled its way down a path through the thick trees, stopping just in front of the capsule. Dark suits poured from the truck like bees from a hive, all carrying crates packed with books.

The young man squinted, trying to make out the titles. Those dark-suited men were not taking away mere rough pages but entire worlds. The men carried the crates toward the entrance of the capsule. One of the doorkeepers pressed a button, and the metal door opened up to an elevator shaft; the smell of the yellowed paper dissipated as the men descended. They were keeping the books, locking them away from everyone. That was their plan; he could see it now. Without books, the men in dark suits could replace thoughts with rules.

***

The Regime's winter made the little room even harder to bear. Shivers had racked his body the night before, both from the chill of the room and the piercing stabs of pain spasming through his left arm. What little sleep he did get was filled with fitful dreams of remorse for his choices and contempt for the dark-suited men.

Being awake was a godsend, despite his aches and pains. The bandage on his left hand was hardened with dried blood, caked to the stinging wound. A tiny window overhead allowed a ray of light, illuminating a small patch of floor next to the bed, but otherwise, Eddington was left in darkness.

Fred came through the door with a plate. Hardened chunks of bread were his only offering. "Help yourself."

Fred untied Eddington, and he collapsed to the floor, his right hand trembling, his left hand throbbing. He crawled over to the bed, searching for any semblance of comfort. Fred helped him along and sat the plate next to him.

"Look, Ed—"

Eddington could barely sit up; his body slumped to the side, his strength depleted. Fred straightened him up and looked into his eyes.

"You will help me to get them back, won't you?"

Eddington nodded.

"I need you now. I really do." The mask of the aggressive torturer dropped, and the layers of treachery were gone. In its place was the face of a lost man.

"What... do you... want... from... from me?"

"Where are they? Please tell me, Ed."

"I don't know."

Fred took in a sharp breath and closed his eyes. He dropped Eddington. "Ed, please."

"I really… don't know…" Eddington struggled and sat back up, head still tilted to the side.

"You've been talking to that man. That one, in the coat? What did he tell you?"

"All about… about The Regime…"

"Yes?" A spark of hope shone through his sunken eyes. As the man furiously scratched his nose, Eddington noticed the pallid yellow of the man's fingernails, stained by years of tobacco use.

"But he never mentioned where the captured go…"

The spark ceased.

"He said something about… this… some reform program. But that's about… about it."

Fred's shoulders sunk. "Anything else?"

Eddington lifted a piece of stale bread. "And I think… I think they kept all the books."

"Who?" The sunken eyes brightened.

"The Regime."

"What? How? Weren't they burned?"

"The… the trucks, Fred? The gray ones… have you… seen them?"

"They go by way too fast. Didn't get a chance." Fred shook his head.

"I think, Fred..." Eddington sat up a little straighter in his bed. His right hand trembled so much that the piece of bread dropped. "I think... there's an archive somewhere..."

"Where is it?"

The tree, the stump, the girl, the trickling stream.

"I don't know."

"You!" Fred pushed Eddington's shoulder. The little tap sent Eddington sprawling back on the bed. Fred grabbed Eddington's collar and pulled him back up. "You go talk to the old man! Find out where it is!"

Eddington stayed quiet. He reached for the piece of bread again.

"You better not be lying to me." Fred stood up, pointing the gun at him again, as casual as if he were just wagging a finger.

Chapter 18

Snow drifted down from the sky, creating a quiet hush over The Regime. Eddington swayed with the wind, limping like a drunkard in the cold. A thin film of white coated the streets, and footprints in straight lines disturbed the perfect serenity. Eddington's blazer wasn't warm enough to protect against the cold, but he couldn't go back to his Complex to get an issued sweater. His hand gripped the bandage, now hardened and dark, as he struggled through the streets, careening his way through the city.

A few students looked at Eddington with confused eyes, but most passed without giving him a second thought. As he shuffled by the café, he tried to hide his face; he'd seen Tom poking around on a glowing screen, and he knew if Tom saw him, his plan would fall apart. But the man must have looked up from his distraction—Eddington could hear his voice shout through the glass.

"Ed!"

Eddington didn't turn his head.

"Come in!"

He was afraid. Afraid that if he sat down in a warm room with his ruined body, he might never get up again. He was on the verge of collapse. Maybe he would slip away, silently, invisibly, if he were too comfortable. His entire body trembled; his breathing was shallow. Tom came out into the snow, his eyes wide and his face wary.

"What in the—"

"The... the..." His teeth chattered. Fred's gun was surely aimed at his head.

"Your hand." Tom leaned over to look.

"Oh... oh..." He gripped onto the bandage tighter, hiding it from Tom. If he stopped, he'd probably die. The steps were the things that kept him alive. The winter's chill was what thrilled his nerves to keep him going. He needed to find Archer.

"Tom... I need to..."

"You need help!"

"No... no... please... I need to..." The streets began to spin. His thoughts were muddled. Somehow, the winter's chill felt warm.

"You should—is that a..." Tom looked to Eddington. There really was something in Tom's eyes: a spark of fear so human and hopeless. It was fleeing, but it stayed just a touch longer that time. He experienced The Cross.

"You need to…" Tom tapped Eddington on the left shoulder. With his weakened body, the tap bowled him over. It almost sunk him into the ground. The sky spun.

The café door swung closed; Eddington and Tom were out in the cold. The street spun.

"Ed?"

Eddington stumbled, weaving as he walked. Even with Tom's hand on his left shoulder, he wavered left and right. His field of view trembled into twisted visions. The snow seemed to melt, and grass sprouted from the concrete pavement. Lampposts turned into trees, and a stream started to trickle through the gutters. He limped with a smile on his face; the cold no longer concerned him. All of his pain dissolved; his limps turned into lightened steps. He knelt down and crumpled to the ground.

"Ed!" Tom tried to catch him but failed. Eddington was planted face down on the pavement. The bandage was torn. Blood began to paint the white snow. He turned over and looked at The Regime's sky with that same smile. Ringing sirens echoed through the streets. Some students stopped walking on the other side of the road to watch. Slowly slipping, he drifted into a spin.

A white van stopped beside him as the siren ceased. A few people with white blazers squashed the thin film of snow with their steps. All he could hear was a string of metal clatters.

"Ed!" Tom was back, but his face was blurred.

Eddington simply smiled. Those in white blazers lifted him up onto the stretcher. His left hand bled over the white sheets.

"How did he…"

"Found him like this. He walked past the café."

"Where have you last…"

"Any…"

Eddington turned his head on the stretcher, still smiling. For a split second, he saw the man with the long dark coat float into an elliptical black blur, trailing amidst the white on the other side of the street. They shoved Eddington into the van, and the dark figure disappeared.

Beep, beep, beep.

His face was covered by a plastic mask. He saw other blurred faces staring down at him.

"Why did…"

"Where to?"

"Sir?"

"The sir?"

"Can't be…"

"Get out, sir; you have to get out!"

He felt those slight vibrations from the sheets of the stretcher. The car was moving.

"Emergency."

"Checkpoint…"

"Ready?"

"His…"

"L'Acad…"

Their faces melted against a dark backdrop. Sterile white lights above Eddington expanded; they were the only sources of brightness in the dark field above his head. The light pulsed, shooting into dim sparkles that rained around him.

"Hello."

Chapter 19

Strides from the young man's brown shoes agitated the stillness of the bookstore. Particles of dust whirled in the air each time he took a step. There were tears in his eyes as he brushed his hands across the shelf that he and Amelia stood in front of when they were younger, giggling and holding hands. The bookstore had shut down, along with all the libraries. A few weeks ago, books were packed into crates, and crates were packed into trucks, and trucks rumbled away. Every book had vanished. Empty shelves, deserted chairs, and tipped tables were the only things left in the bookstore, like scattered tributes at a long-forgotten grave. Spiders and bugs invaded the space, claiming it as their own. The tungsten bulbs overhead sat dark; the store was no longer alive. It was a carcass of a welcoming creature. Stranger still, it was taxidermy—a recreation. You knew what it once was; it was familiar to you, you recognized it, but something was off. Without the spark of life, of animation, of books that bled color into the scene, the bookstore was dead.

The streets were occupied mostly by people with blazers of different colors with the occasional appearance of a militant figure, roaming around masked and armed with machine guns. Humming gray trucks also trailed the streets, carrying crates of bygone worlds. The city was emptied of books, except for his only book left in his hand. They'd never take that away from him.

It was only the beginning. A few days before, the young man saw buses packed with people in blazers carried out of the city. No one ever told him where they were going or why they were sent away. All he knew was they were never seen again. Black-suited men known as "Prefects" patrolled the area where he lived, constantly questioning every move of every person who walked the streets. He was under constant surveillance, and even though the deserted bookstore was a restricted area, the young man didn't care. He carried the book and retraced memories along the aisles, and a teardrop fell from his eye and landed on the dusty floor. He walked toward the large window overlooking the street; a few people in navy blazers roamed under the setting sun.

He thought of her again—of the outlines and wide smiles with crinkled eyes—as he neared the window.

He closed his eyes, and as he opened them, his vision blurred. A bus hurried past, and a few more tears fell. He got closer to the window, set the book down, and touched the glass with both of his hands.

The young man took a deep breath, and a broad smile appeared as he looked into the sunset. A sensation ballooned within as he pressed his palms against the window. A series of spasms contracted and relaxed his airway as laughter, actual laugher, echoed through the dead space.

Fingers against the cold, fogged glass. Face ridden with tears not dried. Air imbued with whirling dust. The door behind the young man burst open as a series of hurried steps agitated more of the layered dust. Bugs skittered back into their hiding spots as the black suits rushed into the bookstore.

"What is that…"

"Sir… you are in…"

"Restricted."

"Arrest."

"Identity?"

"Vari…"

"Abort?"

"Special…"

The laughter never ceased. It echoed through the space against the backdrop of the tensed black suits.

"Immediate?"

"Sir…"

"Execute."

"Branch?"

"Unbranched."

"Number?"

The young man turned around, face bright with a beaming smile. The Prefects stood frozen; one of them was holding a black cloth bag.

Walk with me.

You should be a poet…

Who are you anyway?

Didn't see her; she was supposed to show up for her shift…

Ed!

Who are you anyway?

One of the black suits took a step toward him.

Father was arrested.

Oh, she works at The Plant.

Beyond the wall…

The black suit came closer and closer, and the young man's laughter was muffled as a bag was shoved over his head. Bugs cautiously came out of their hiding spots as the men stomped out of the store, settling back on the shelves of the deserted bookstore.

***

Beep.

The room was entirely white, as if all color had been sucked from every surface. Nurses were dressed in white, the walls were white, the bedsheets were white. No adornment livened the place; Eddington felt empty, just like the room. A monitor on Eddington's left went *beep, beep, beep.*

He lay there as traces of pain pinned him to the sheets. His mind was quite muddled from all that had happened. Everything felt like a twisted dream, but the new bandage on his left hand suggested otherwise. He was unable to move his body; even taking a deep breath in pained his chest. His mind raced with questions unsolved. His consciousness dipped in and out. All that remained was a name with a familiar ring.

Amelia.

His hands gripped the starched sheets. His face contorted in pain. He tried to get out of bed, but his body still ached.

The door swung open, and a Prefect came in.

"Sir, are you feeling better?"

Eddington nodded.

"Standard portioned meal, sir."

The Prefect left a silver packet on the little table on the right-hand side of the bed.

"Also, you have a visitor."

The Prefect left the room. Almost immediately, Archer stepped in, his coat resting on his left arm.

"Ed?"

Eddington tried to sit up at the sight of Archer, but the aches and pains hurtling through his body restricted his movement.

"Hold still." Archer steadied Eddington and gently pressed him back to the bed. "You need to rest so you can recover soon." Archer walked over to the window and overlooked the snowy scene. "Bastards."

Eddington looked at Archer, his eyes wide at the remark.

"Who did this to you?" Archer turned around.

There was a sliver of silence.

"Bloody Rogues." Archer turned back to the view at the window while his right hand tapped the frame. "They'll all get rounded up."

"Rounded up?" Eddington muttered, his words strung together by the barest of threads, his thoughts scrambling in his head too fast for him to catch. "What... round... round up?"

"The Rogues? Yes."

"Where... to...?"

Archer took a deep breath and turned to Eddington. "Ed, you still don't understand. You—"

A Prefect ghosted in.

"Sir, your time is up."

"Thank you." Archer slipped into his long coat and edged toward the door. "Get better soon. You need to recover."

Archer walked out, and the Prefect left with him. Eddington sat in the blank room, alone.

Chapter 20

Weeks passed. Maybe a month. They confined Eddington to the little white room, helping him heal and telling him nothing. He was trapped, both physically and mentally—there were no books to read or pages to write on.

He recovered gradually. The once-gaping wound on his left hand congealed into a dark-brown scab as the nurses changed the bandages around the clock. They treated the whip wounds with some kind of ointment that eased the pain. A Man of Medicine came in often. He said he recognized Eddington. They'd probably met at the café.

Throughout the weeks, he worked on getting back onto his feet and pacing around the room. At times he looked through the window at the courtyard draped in snow. The only things that stood out were the black fences and the tall entrance gate.

About a month into his recovery, the Prefects granted him his first walk out in the courtyard. They gave him a warm coat and told him to explore, but they watched his every move. The building, he was surprised to find out, was rather old: ivy crawled up the gray stone façade, and large windows peered out to the lawn below. It occurred to him that the building must have been a family estate long before it had ever been a hospital. The path Eddington walked on sliced through the grounds, and though it was a sunny day, the snow refused to melt.

Eddington circled the courtyard around and around. The Prefects stood still as lampposts in front of the entrance. Despite their presence, he was feeling better. The whip wounds had healed, and a dark, black scab was beginning to form on the finger without a fingernail. He veered from the path and stepped on the snow; it made a crunching sound. The noise reached into his memory, much like how his episodes of dreams reminded him of his past. Another step, another crunch.

He'd been with his father on a snowy mountain peak. He was still quite young then. His father had to help him with his skis, though the ever-present cigarette still hung from the man's mouth. In Eddington's memory, his father didn't speak much, but his smile and quick wit always charmed Eddington.

Another step, another crunch.

He heard it again. That time it was in the woods during winter. Eddington had on a puffer jacket along with a thick pair of gloves and walked along the frozen stream. The ice was solid beneath his feet. The branches near the stream were burdened with layers of white. He walked; the snow crunched. She threw; the snowball scattered on the back of Eddington's puffer jacket. Startled, he turned around and saw the giggling girl in a red beanie. He blushed. The girl ran over and embraced him in a tight hug.

Amelia.

Eddington looked up at the sky in front of the hospital. He smiled at the clouds. The Prefect came over.

"Sir, your time's up."

Another two weeks passed as Eddington circulated from the room to the courtyard, from the courtyard to the restroom, and from the restroom back to the white bed.

Endless, monotonous addition.

It was toward the end of the second week that Eddington received a notice of return. He was well enough to be transferred back to District-E. As he woke up that morning, agitation washed over him. It was still quite dark; the sun was nothing more than an orange sliver on the distant horizon, bleeding tinges of crimson into the dark blue sky. He sat and listened to his own breathing. The sun slowly rose behind the cloudless plain, enlivening the scene out Eddington's window.

Eddington was dressed in his blazer and was ready to go. Later rather than sooner, the door swung open as Archer and a Prefect walked in.

"Feeling all right?" Archer had his overcoat on, seemingly ready to depart with Eddington.

Eddington didn't say anything. He stood up from the bed and walked toward the door, passing the Prefect and Archer without a nod.

"Ed." Archer pursued Eddington and reached for his shoulder.

Eddington turned around. "You're with The Regime."

"Yes. Wasn't that obvious?"

"Lies."

Eddington exited his room and strode along the corridor of the old hospital.

"Ed, listen!"

"Rogues, The Archive, The Double-Rods, the buds—all blatant lies."

"It works."

"It works?" Eddington turned around and looked at Archer squarely in the eyes. "Yeah, it works. People going on and on. Thinking they know everything when, in fact, they know nothing!"

"And people don't want to know anyway!"

"People do. But you round them up."

"Listen, you can't have everyone running on their own terms."

"So, what, this Regime turns them into robots? Round and round, from L'Académie to home, then take The Box again to L'Académie? Is this a true education to you? Who even are you?"

Archer's shoulders sunk. He looked at the floor, plunged in thought, then turned to the Prefect and waved him away.

"Take a walk with me, Ed."

***

Eddington saw Archer's trembling right hand. The two were seated on a wooden bench. It was quite cold out. Both were wrapped in winter coats; Eddington in a checkered pattern of brown and tan, Archer in black.

"Another lap?"

"I don't mind."

The two got up; the silence was broken by the crunching snow beneath their feet. Archer glanced at the young man's face once in a while. Eddington simply walked and looked down at the snow. The tension carried on for a few more laps. Upon their return to the bench, Eddington spoke. "You were about to say something."

Archer sat down on the bench; his once assured gaze took on a tint of sorrow. Eddington didn't like seeing Archer in that light.

"Ed, sit."

"We've been doing that for a while, haven't we?"

Archer stood back up and sighed. He patted Eddington on the back and started pacing around the yard. Archer reminded Eddington of himself when he first met Amelia. Shuffling back and forth, walking laps through the same dull tracks over and over, not daring to air the words he wanted to say. The suspense annoyed him.

"You know, I liked that forest too."

Eddington's eyes widened.

"How did you…" Eddington placed his hands in his pockets and took a step back from Archer.

"That forest? How would I not." Archer paused. "The Archive. The Archive is in *that* forest." Perhaps it was a realization—or a hesitation.

"Why are you telling me this?"

"I thought you—wanted to know."

"I already knew."

"You remember?"

"Pieces of it." Eddington gave Archer a brief glance and turned toward the main gate. "If there's nothing else, I'll have to go."

"Ed!"

A dark van was parked in front of the building. Two Prefects came out and opened the door for Eddington.

"Ed!"

Eddington simply ducked into the van with his long, checkered coat still on; the Prefects halted Archer's steps.

"Sir, please step back."

"Right. Right."

"Let him go, sir. We'll keep an eye on him."

"Keep him safe. Keep him away from those bastards." Archer furrowed his brows.

"We'll try, sir."

Eddington was plunged into a sea of incoherent thoughts as he sat in the van. The windows were blacked out; he could only hear the humming engine and feel the bumpy road.

The two Prefects drove without speaking. Eddington had expected the van to continue on to his Complex, but they'd stopped. He still couldn't see out, but the Prefect in the driver's seat rolled down the window and grunted to the guard standing outside. It must have been a checkpoint, but they passed without fuss. The dark tinge on the window slowly lightened, revealing a district that looked all too familiar. It drove past L'Académie's square, the café, the backstreets, the alleyways, Bay Seven of the Boxes' station.

That was beyond The Wall.

He realized the hospital was on the other side of the wall.

I was beyond The Wall.

Soon, the Prefects parked in front of Eddington's Complex. He got out and walked straight to the staircase, where he paused. The engine's rumble faded in the distance. Eddington remained at the staircase's entrance for a while. All he could think about was one thing. All his agitated ways sought but one relief. All the mysteries resided in one place.

The Archive is in the forest.

At that instant, tender laughter interrupted Eddington's thoughts. He turned and saw a boy and a girl with their blazers off, chattering with each other in a backstreet. They were the ones who held hands before on the curb. Eddington approached them.

"What are you two doing here?" He heard his own mechanical voice.

They froze.

"Get a move on."

They got up hastily and ran back out to the street. Eddington smiled at the tattered steps of the two as he recalled his own little encounters, little banters, and little slivers of laughter with Amelia.

Chapter 21

Fred was a wrangled beast locked up in a squalid cage. Eddington remembered the rancid smell and the hideous hideout. Flashbacks of the dim tungsten blub and the painful whips made him flinch; all that came from a man once composed and calm. What lived in the hideout was not human, but something—or rather, some *thing*—to scare away visitors with its madness. Some *thing* that might pull out another nail of his. Some *thing* forever altered by grief.

He was in front of that door he'd once loved and later loathed. Once the entrance to a place he considered home, later a room of confined torture. He knocked and shoved his hands back into his coat pockets to ward against the chill.

He heard footsteps from inside of the door, which made him uneasy. Those steps no longer sounded like footsteps. It was a series of hurried tatters, bobbing, struggling, and possibly crawling with the strength it had left. The handle turned, and the door opened. Eddington took a step back.

His eyes were sunken, and his cheekbones were sharp against the thin layer of pale skin on his face. He'd lost so much weight with nothing to eat, without Joe's talent for finding scraps. That slight hunch to his back made him look a decade older.

He coughed. All Eddington could smell was tobacco.

"Where"—he wheezed—"have you been, fool's boy?"

Fred's voice was weak and scratchy.

"God damn it, you." He pointed a finger at Eddington. "The Regime. You're cruel, cruel people."

Eddington stood there with a blank face. "I know where it is now."

Fred's eyes brightened. "Ah! Where"—Fred rasped—"is it?"

"Somewhere only I know." He took another step away from Fred.

"Oh, boy—forgive me! Forgive me!" Fred began to sob as he rushed up to Eddington and grabbed his shoulders. "Oh! I was so wretched! Thank you, my friend."

Eddington struggled out of his grip and dusted himself off. "But we can't get there now."

"Why not?" Fred took a step toward him as another fit of coughing shook his twig of a frame.

"I don't know how to get there, but…"

"But what?"

"Maybe the trucks do."

"The gray ones?" Fred widened his eyes.

"They carry the books to The Archive. Maybe we could tail it."

"You…" Flamed passion filled Fred. His tremoring hand pulled out the gun. "You want me gone too, eh? Prefects on trucks, and you can just"—he wheezed—"hand me over, eh?"

"No." Eddington's hands remained in the pockets of the checkered coat. "Take it or leave it." He swung around, waiting for Fred to follow, and walked toward the main street. After a few steps, he heard crisp metal clatters echo throughout the alleyway of the hideout: the sound of a gun dropped on bare concrete.

The door of the café swung open, and Eddington walked in.

"Ed!" Tom stood up from his seat and looked at Eddington with puzzled eyes.

Eddington closed the door behind him and sat across from Tom. "Don't."

"Don't what?" Tom sat back down to his seat.

"Don't annoy me with your rambles, please." Eddington smiled.

"That's the thing, man." Tom took a sip out of his cup. "What happened to you? The other day. Man, that was scary lookin'. Your hand, your face."

"Told you, had a bit of an accident."

"An accident? Ha! I know better. By the way, nice coat." Tom straightened himself in his chair and peeked out of the window. Eddington looked at Tom and smiled again.

"Thank you."

"Where's your blazer, huh? Sick of it? You know those Prefects might not be too happy." Tom's gaze was not at the window, not what was just past the window, but farther, as if his focus was miles—or worlds—away.

"I don't know. Left it at the hospital."

"Are you well put together now? Your finger is still..." Tom didn't want to look at Eddington's left hand.

"Yeah, fine." Eddington looked down at the dark scab. "Still breathing."

That glimmer of what was human came through Tom's eyes again. The two looked at one another. They both laughed, startling those who were used to a silent café.

"So, that day, what happened? You were out there! About to die!"

"Sir." Eddington raised his brows. "You are asking a prohibited question."

"Since when did you talk like one of them now?" Tom punched Eddington on the shoulder.

"Since when do you speak like a Rogue now?" As Eddington leaned back from the punch, another burst of laughter rang through the café.

"Well." Tom took another sip out of the cup and leaned toward Eddington, speaking in a lowered voice. "I found, uh, a book."

"You did what?" Eddington's face froze as he screwed up his brows.

"I found a book." Tom looked out the window again. No Prefect walked past.

"No." Eddington leaned back.

"There was this book... That guy's brilliant, simply brilliant. You know those Parisian cafés, right? Where people sit and fine ladies pass by?"

Eddington didn't know what to make of it.

"Yeah. Bullfights, Spain, Paris..." He kept his voice low.

"Do you know what this means, Tom?" Eddington whispered.

"But what's that gonna do?" Tom looked out the window again. Eddington noticed the Man of History no longer wore the earbuds. "I'm getting this sense, man"—Tom turned his eyes back to Eddington—"that L'Académie is feeding us—"

"You've been *skipping*?" Eddington widened his eyes.

"Evidently." A little smirk appeared on his face.

"Tom, don't. You'll—"

"Get in trouble?" He crossed his arms.

"I don't want them to get you."

"They won't." Tom lifted his cup and drank from it. "I'm never going back in there."

"Where?" Eddington leaned in. "Where did you put the book?"

"Hidden away. Safe as ever." Tom smiled.

"Well." Eddington looked around the café; no one seemed to pay attention to their conversation. "Stay low." Eddington patted Tom on one shoulder as he stood back up. "I'll be back later."

"Later, Ed." He was still smiling.

After exiting the café, Eddington took a few turns and arrived at Fred's hideout.

"Fred?" He knocked on the door and listened for the footsteps.

"Ye—yes?"

"What did they do to your books?" Eddington recalled that when Fred confined him, there were ripped pages of books on the floor.

"They robbed me! They came in and robbed me! Cruel bastards!" Eddington heard a string of steps pacing the room behind the door. "Why are you here now? Where are they? Where are they captured?"

"I'm not sure." Eddington took a step back from the door, afraid that Fred might rush out with a gun again. "Fred..."

"No! *You try to bring me to them!*" Fred screamed through the door.

"Fred! Listen!"

Cries mingled with muffled words came through the closed door. Eddington could no longer understand the majority of those words.

"Crazy." Eddington reentered the café and saw Tom staring into space. "Hey!"

"Huh?" Tom started, and it took him a second for him to recognize Eddington in his checkered coat. "Where've you..."

"Not here." Eddington looked around the café.

"What do you mean?" Tom's gaze followed Eddington's.

"Follow me." Eddington darted to the backdoor that led to the courtyard. Tom looked out of the café's window one more time before scrambling after him. The café without the two was completely empty.

"Why are we out here?" Tom shivered out in the cold without a coat.

"Nowhere else to go. Ada said this was a blind spot."

"Who's—oh, her."

"She was captured. God knows where she went." Eddington rubbed his palms.

"So." Tom paced around, trying to warm up. "Why am I here?"

"Where's that book?"

"What do you mean?" Tom looked at him, still not out of his daze.

"I mean, where did you get it?" Eddington said.

"It was scattered near this alleyway, and I picked it up," Tom said. "There was a bunch of other rubbish around it too. Prefects weren't around, so I—"

"Do you have it with you?" Eddington said.

Tom shrugged and reached into his blazer. After looking around and hunching his back, he handed his book to Eddington, who caressed the cover.

"What are you doing?" Tom tried to get the book back, but it was too late. Eddington dropped it into a humming garbage processing unit, where it was chopped to pieces.

"You're mad!" Tom rushed up to Eddington and wrenched his shoulder back, forcing him closer to the wall.

"No. If I hadn't done that, they'd—"

"They'd what? Arrest me?" Tom shoved him again.

"Keep it down." Eddington placed his finger to his lips.

"But my book!" Tom said.

"You don't understand."

"Ed, you…"

"You're with The Regime!"

Eddington was back at the alley of the hideout after his brawl with Tom.

"Are there any more they missed?" Eddington shouted through the door.

"I don't know! They robbed me! If they missed something, I wouldn't know!" Fred kept the door shut.

"Listen, Fred. If you want to get them back, we have to know what this Archive thing—"

"You're with that black coat! He took them away!" Fred shouted.

"Fred! You're—"

The door swung open.

"Back off! Back off!" Fred's shaky hand gripped the gun.

"Look." Hands in the air, Ed slowly backed out of Fred's doorway. "You're not the only one."

"One what?" Fred tried to steady his hand with the gun.

Amelia.

"They also took someone away from me." Eddington kept his hands in the air. "I need to understand, Fred. When they robbed your place, where did they put the books?"

Fred still had the gun up, but his anger had calmed. "I, I don't—"

"Come on, Fred." Eddington took a step closer to the opened door. "When you saw them breaking down your door, where did they take your books?"

"I…" Fred's shoulders sunk.

Chapter 22

The chill winter in The Regime still lingered. A few people wandered the streets, but most stayed inside, warming themselves against the stark wind. The little couple Eddington had seen before cuddled in a back alleyway. A humming van screeched to a stop in front of them, and two Prefects stepped out.

Only snippets of muttered conversation could be heard. "No, it's not…"

"Please…"

The door of the van closed. The boy and the girl disappeared from the streets. They'd never be seen holding hands and cuddling again.

Across the street, Archer overlooked the entire thing. He hadn't shaved in a while. The stubbles aged him, deepening the lines on his face and giving him an unkempt appearance. He sighed, shook his head, and took a turn into the café. The café was empty on that day. He didn't take his coat off, and he wasn't really in the mood for a cup of coffee either. He went over to the bar and pressed something on the screen—a drink was served, though no money was exchanged.

His face mellowed under the burn of the drink sliding down his throat. He had a few more sips and leaned against the bar counter. He sighed again as the tension eased. From the reflection of his drinking glass, he saw someone enter the café.

"Last week, you said?" Eddington asked.

"Yes, indeed. Two were taken again." Tom nodded.

"Was that the van that—"

Eddington stopped the second he saw Archer at the bar. His hands still remained in his checkered coat pockets. Archer turned around and smiled that same smile.

"Hi, Ed."

"Why are you here?" Eddington's right hand tremored a little.

"I was going to tell you, but you left." Archer shrugged and began walking toward Eddington.

"You were beating around the bush," Eddington said, his gaze wary as he stepped back.

"I can't just tell you up front. Feeling better?" He raised his brows.

"Better than ever." Eddington held eyes with Archer.

Tom shuffled his eyes between the two.

"You saw that little couple outside." A smirk appeared on Archer's face.

"Quite proud of it?"

"No." Archer laughed under his intoxicated fit. "No! I had to."

"You didn't." Eddington shook his head.

"My God! Eddington!" Archer smashed the whiskey glass on the café's floor. Tom started.

"Then why? Why did you?" Eddington kept shaking his head.

"Look at yourself. Are you really one of them? The Rogues? One of the good ones? Fighting for the purity of Jesus or some shit? You would've been gone without me a long time ago!" Archer was red-faced.

"Why me?" Eddington's right hand starting tremoring again. "Just who are you?"

Tears swelled in Archer's eyes. "No, that's not the question!"

"Then what is?" A hint of anger was in Eddington's voice.

"You—" Archer pointed at Tom.

Two Prefects came into the café. One of them carried a black cloth bag.

"Tom? No, you can't!"

"I'm sorry. We've had our eyes on him for a while now." Archer pulled the tattered copy of the book Eddington had disposed of from his coat, the edges worn and some of the cover torn. "He's been up to no good, Ed. And you knew it. Good, very good. Three in a row."

"Three?"

"Ed!" Tom struggled in their grip. Soon his voice was muffled by a black bag over his head.

"You really think you're in control? You really think you can get away with those neat little tricks played by the Rogues? Think again." Archer dropped the ruined book on the wooden floor.

"You!" Eddington rushed toward the two Prefects, trying to separate Tom from their grip. Another black suit rushed into the café and ripped Eddington away from the conflict.

"You, on the other hand. You're safe. You got away. Ever wondered why?"

"No! Let him go!"

"You never wondered? You little rascal. Why allow you to read? Oh, I know why." Archer took a deep breath, a grin appearing on his face. "You remember now, do you? She was quite a sweet little thing; I'll give you that. What was her name? Oh, she was lovely. Amelia, was it?"

"You!" Eddington struggled out of the grip of the Prefect and rushed toward Archer. He grabbed the black collar of his long overcoat. "Where is she? *Where is she?* What have you done to her?"

"Whoa, don't get too ahead of yourself." The grin made him look garish. "You know the other two? Ada and Joe? Well, they'll be back to The Regime real soon. Quite changed. Quite obedient now. They probably won't even remember you at all."

"What have you done with them?" Eddington shook Archer.

"What this gentleman will soon go through." He pointed at Tom with the black bag over his head. "Take him out."

"No!" Eddington shoved Archer against the bar. Bottles clinked on the shelf behind.

"Oh, dear. Got something left in you, huh?" Archer smirked. A Prefect showed up behind Eddington and pulled him away from Archer. "Wild thoughts, Eddington." Archer dusted himself. "You've tried. Take them both!"

A bag slipped over Eddington's head.

"Sir?" the Prefect said.

"Yes?"

"You might want to—"

A loud bang rang out as a bottle shattered. A heavy thud followed; Eddington was relieved of the grip.

"What in the devil?"

"O! Angels above! O, Holy Savior!"

Through the fabric of the bag, Eddington could see Fred holding his gun with a shaky hand as he pointed it at Archer.

"Get thee behind me! Devil! Thou lurking serpent!"

"What on the wild earth are—"

Another loud bang.

"Stay, you two!" Archer ordered the Prefects still holding Tom.

"Let the two young men go." Fred's hand trembled but still pointed the gun squarely at Archer.

"Who are you?" Archer had his hands in the air.

"Don't know me, eh?" Fred slowly walked toward Archer to the point where the cold barrel was right against Archer's forehead. "You knew the other two. Brilliant, bloody brilliant."

"How did you…"

Fred looked over at Eddington with a grin. "I was listening."

"Listen. Killing me won't solve a thing. The two are already—"

"Shut your mouth!" Fred began to sob. "You... fucking... monster. This place, this system. Don't you see? Learning? Or are you engineering slaves?"

"Stability." Archer tilted his head up, giving them all a strange smile.

Another bang. Blood splattered across Archer's face. Fred was shot through his left arm as he fell to the ground, groaning in pain.

Eddington's sob was muffled by the bag, still stuffed over his head.

"O! You wretched fiend! Begone!" Fred clenched his teeth as he fell. But with the strength he had left, Fred pressed himself up and gave out two more shots. The two Prefects gripping Tom fell to the ground, reddening the wooden floor of the café.

"Run, you two!" Fred shouted.

Eddington took the bag off Tom's head, and they ran toward the exit.

Archer cleared his throat. "You're dead."

A red laser spot showed up on the back of Fred's head. Fred smiled at Archer. Another loud bang. Fred's head dangled as his body went limp. A trail of hurried footsteps was printed on the snow outside the café, leading to a side alleyway.

Chapter 23

"What in the wild was—"

"Fred!" Eddington tried to catch up with his short-lived breath. "He's…"

"Captured?"

"Good chance he's dead."

"Oh." Tom rubbed his palms while staring at the snow-covered ground. "Dead?"

"Yes. Dead. Like we'll be soon."

"Died—someone died at the bull ring."

"What?"

"Nothing."

The two were in an alleyway. Eddington leaned against a wall while Tom continued to rub his palms and pace around in circles, mumbling. "Dead. He's dead." All of a sudden, he said, "Who was he? That man?"

"Rogue." Eddington closed his eyes.

"Wait, that was a Rogue? Why did he—"

"Tom." Eddington pushed himself away from the wall. "How long have you been out of L'Académie?"

"A few weeks."

"Do you remember anything from there?"

"Uh... Law of Suspects, seventeen ninety-three? Don't know the month."

"What was it?"

"Something about the French Revolution."

"It's fading away, I see." Eddington sighed. "It disappears quite quickly if you don't go there, doesn't it?"

"But people in that book—they never left me." Tom looked around as if even the mention of a book could get him arrested.

"Oh. What book was it?"

"The one that got me in trouble back there." He took a deep breath. "I just—now that all that stuff is fading away, I don't know what to do."

"If we can get out—" Eddington paused. *Out.* It sounded so foreign. "But before that happened at the bar, you told me you saw the gray trucks."

"Guarded. Saw them a few days ago."

"You said they come once every few weeks, correct?" Eddington said.

"I don't know. I'm not so sure." Tom stopped pacing around.

"You did see one the other day, you said."

"Yeah. What about it, though?" Tom kept on rubbing his palms. "Why are you so obsessed with where the trucks are going?"

"They go to The Archive." Eddington had his eyes fixed on the other end of the alleyway.

"Why does it matter? A man was shot back there!"

"I thought you knew all about it. Eh? Two months, you'd be out. Beyond The Wall." Eddington fixed his eyes on Tom.

"I thought I did too." Tom looked down at the prints he left as he walked in circles a minute before. "But that book, man. That damned book."

"Damned?" Eddington raised his brows.

"What, is that a prohibited word?" Tom said.

"I was just wondering where you picked it up." Eddington looked away from Tom and looked out of the alleyway again.

"Who was that man? In the long coat?"

"Archer." Eddington fumbled through his coat's empty pockets as he shivered.

"He knew all about you?" Tom said.

"That's the thing. I don't trust him at all."

"But then—"

"Tom." Eddington buttoned up his checkered coat. "We can't stay here for long. We're technically fugitives now. They'll be looking for us."

"We're what?"

"We're Rogues."

The two took the back way into Eddington's Complex—the normal way would cross paths with the armored guards along The Wall. They snuck up the staircase and entered Eddington's dark room.

"This is it? Your screens are broken?" Tom tried to feel his way through the dark.

"One day, they just decided to turn off." Eddington took off his coat and began cleaning up all the scattered pages.

"You wrote all of that?"

"Somewhat." Eddington gathered the two books that were on the ground and placed them on the living room table. Tom picked up one of the books. "For a long time, I used to go to bed quite early."

Tom was wide-eyed as he stared at the ink on the page. "This is what you spend your time doing now?"

"Better than horsing around at L'Académie. We need to hurry." Eddington looked up at the cameras.

"Take these with us?" Tom held up the book in his hand.

"Yes, yes. Swiftly now."

Eddington cracked the door of the apartment open.

"Anyone?" Tom whispered.

"A Chemistry guy."

The door shut as Eddington and Tom ducked back into the apartment.

"Wait for him to pass. Then, old way in, old way out. I don't want the guards after us."

A string of ordered steps passed by the closed door of Eddington's unit.

"Right, he's in. Remember: old way in, old way out."

Tom gripped the two heavy books and snuck down the staircase while Eddington followed. They avoided the path crossing The Wall and ended up on a backstreet.

"Here, this way."

A few turns away, they ended up at the garbage processing yard where Eddington had first met Archer.

"Through here," Eddington said.

They hurried through the kitchen area and ended up at the staircase leading up to the Victorian apartment with the red carpet.

"Where are you taking me?" Tom said.

"You think I have a clue?" It was but a movement of habit. A straight path he knew how to follow. They entered the old apartment with carpeted floors and strange wallpaper, and Tom lingered for a few moments before opening up the door to the hallway. "What are you looking at?" He stopped as he saw Tom's stare.

"I've never seen a place like this."

"I thought so too," Eddington whispered. "Follow! We don't have time."

Sprinkles of snow melted into the carpet of the hallway, leaving behind damp footprints. Eddington and Tom reached the staircase that descended to Archer's cellar.

"What is this?"

"Cellar door." Eddington twisted the bar, and the door opened. Smashed shelves and scattered furniture and books torn apart—all unchanged since the last time he had been there.

"That freak lived here?"

"Would you stop asking me questions?" Eddington shouted as he fumbled through the scattered furniture. "Prohibited! Prohibited! Prohibited!"

"Well, you're not with The Regime anymore, are you?"

"Nor are you." Eddington turned to Tom for a second. "The Man of History…"

Eddington continued to look through the squalid room in hopes of finding something that would make sense of the mess he was in.

The Archive is in the forest.

Eddington shook his head.

You should be a poet!

Eddington's eyes squeezed shut.

Walk. Walk with me.

Eddington stood straight up; his right hand began to tremor.

Amelia!

Eddington covered his face with both of his hands.

You're with The Regime!

"Stop it!" Eddington kicked one of the chairs scattered across the room.

"Whoa!" Tom jumped. The chair slid and clattered against the wall, rattling until it rested on its side.

"Don't!" Eddington's squeezed his eyes shut. "Don't!"

You lurking serpent!

Get thee behind me!

Go, you two!

"Fred," Tom said.

"Sorry?" Eddington opened his eyes. Images flashed across his mind: Fred, greeting him in a rumpled sweater; his calming presence next to the barrel of fire; his slow descent into madness. "He's dead..."

"Yes, he is." Tom still held on to the two heavy books. "What *is* this?"

"Grief." Eddington looked Tom in the eyes.

Silence remained in the room. The two looked at one another as if they just awakened from a hideous dream into a grosser reality. They were alone. Aimless. Nowhere to go and nowhere to attach themselves to. The only remedy was to go beyond The Wall—to go into The Archive. That was the only thing left to do.

Chapter 24

The darkening sky painted the clouds in bright oranges and a tinge of purple. Two men, one in a gray blazer, the other in a checkered overcoat, overlooked The Regime from a rooftop.

"Beautiful, ain't it." Tom broke the silence.

"Ain't it?" Eddington turned to him. "You sound like... like Joe."

"Who's Joe?"

"One of the people they took away."

"Three in a row, eh? I was the third?" Tom turned to Eddington.

"Lucky you weren't."

The two men continued to look out across a Regime they were once familiar with. At that moment, they were above it all. But they knew it was only temporary.

"Now, here's what I don't get." Eddington spoke without turning his head. "What changed? You could've stayed at the café and kept up with L'Académie. What happened?"

"Sir." Tom cleared his throat; there was a twinkle in his eyes despite his serious tone. "That's a prohibited question."

"No, really. What changed?" He turned a sharp gaze onto Tom.

"I don't know. It was weird. Don't even remember how I got the copy. It didn't make sense at first, but gradually…"

"What?" Eddington took a step toward him.

"The book just took me." Tom shrugged.

"Right." A nod.

Another sliver of silence.

"What is this Archive anyway?" Tom turned to Eddington.

"Think of this…" Eddington grabbed the two books Tom was clutching and held them up. "But a whole lot of them. All of them, in fact, held up somewhere."

"Is that what it is?"

"At least that's what I've heard." Eddington gave back the books. "Lots of books housed in an Archive. Every book, they said."

"Huh." The spark of an idea appeared in Tom's eyes. "The Plant!"

"Exactly. They feed the books through to L'Académie. Fed them to us. Like regurgitated slop."

"Why don't they just teach the books?"

"Ha!" Eddington laughed. "No one reads."

"I do!"

"You know enough from L'Académie already. You don't need books."

"But they fade, like... Robespierre? Only remember the name."

"He was the man with the large jaw. It was shot through days before his execution. Guillotined around seventeen ninety-four—something about a conspiracy."

"How did you remember that? I can only remember that he was the leader of The Terror."

"I've read it," Eddington said.

"So, you're saying if you read something, you'll remember it?" Tom said.

"Only the relevant stuff, really. The things that change the way you look at the world."

"Ah!" Tom clicked his fingers. "The Cross!"

"There you are." Eddington's mouth curled into a faint smile.

The sun was submerged under the sky's horizon. The tint of bright orange had faded; only a hint of purple lingered beyond the buildings.

"What are we going to do? We'll be dead pretty soon, eh?" Tom said.

"We'll rob the Archive." Eddington's faint smile remained. "We'll rob it, and we'll get out. Screw this place."

"What?" Tom's eyes widened. "Rob it?"

"And you thought I was so wrapped up with the trucks."

***

They slept in the staircase that night. It was the crack of dawn; humming sounds came from the street below. Tom urged Eddington out of the staircase, and the two ended up on the rooftop, looking down into the streets.

"The… the truck," Tom said.

"There it is." Eddington's eyes were fixed on the Prefects.

Below, a few black suits stormed the building. The rest guarded the truck.

"You ready?" Eddington whispered.

"Wait, what?" Tom whipped his head.

Eddington ducked into the staircase and pulled a wayward iron rod from the banister.

"What good is that going to do?" Tom uttered as he followed Eddington down the staircase. His voice echoed in the stairway.

"Give The Regime a good blow." Eddington looked at Tom with the rod in his hand. There was the beginning of a smile on his face.

Chapter 25

Light streaming from the windows illuminated the hallway. Eddington stood still, overlooking the long stretch of space. On the left, a row of doors along the wall led to more rooms. On the right, light shone through, casting rectangles on the floor. He heard footsteps coming from below the staircase, so he quickly retreated into one of the doors on his left. He gripped the metal rod tighter and leaned his head out of the doorway: two black-suited figures were roaming about with empty crates in their hands. They went into the first room of the corridor and came out a little later with heavier crates. He could hear their footsteps tramp down the stairs. The truck continued its hum.

Tom waited to make sure the Prefects carried on with their downward march until he tiptoed down the steps toward Eddington. He peeked out the doorway and felt a tug on the back of his jacket. "Shh…" Eddington said as he pulled Tom into the room.

More footsteps ascended from the distant stairs. The two Prefects returned carrying empty crates. They went into the second room of the corridor, fumbling about with muffled thuds.

"What in the world are they doing?" Tom said.

"Garbage season," Eddington uttered.

"Books are still around?"

"In nooks and crannies. Hidden, forgotten, or thrown away." Eddington clenched the metal rod in his hand. The Prefects exited the second room and went downstairs.

"How are we going to do this?"

"I've got a plan." Eddington looked at his metal rod.

"But…" Tom was still gripping the two books. "What if?" The number of ways he could end the question swirled between the two men.

"Got a better idea?" Eddington gave him a look.

The footsteps ascended the stairs again. Tom and Eddington retreated farther back into the room as the two dark suits entered the third door along the corridor.

"How come I didn't know?" Tom whispered.

"Maybe it's ongoing. Books aren't going to go away overnight. There are still loads of them around."

Muffled thuds and bangs grew louder. The Prefects soon went out of the room with two full crates.

"What's your damn plan?" Tom was rubbing his palms.

"You'll see."

The truck continued to hum. The two carriers with crates came up the stairs again and went into the fourth room.

"You sure the truck goes to The Archive?"

"Maybe." Eddington wrapped himself tighter in his overcoat.

The thuds from the falling books grew louder. The Prefects traipsed downstairs again, back to the humming gray truck.

"Okay." A determined look sparked in his eyes. "Anything in the bathroom?" Eddington tested the strength of the rod by pressing it against his shin.

"Hmm." Tom went into the bathroom of the room and opened a cabinet. The footsteps from the stairs grew louder. The Prefects were in the neighboring room to Eddington, and Tom fumbled his way to an orange canister with a black spider printed on the side and a nozzle on the top. "Oh, geez, what the hell is…" *Cough.*

The muffled thuds next door stopped. Eddington and Tom held their breath.

"Continue," a voice said. The muffled thuds resumed.

"God," Eddington wheezed. "That'll do." He squeezed his nose as he patted Tom on the shoulder.

A string of footsteps exited the room next door. The Prefects with their crates descended the stairs and went back to the gray humming truck.

"We're next," Eddington said with a shaky voice. "You hide in the bathroom and spray them, and I'll—"

"You're mad!" Tom gasped, trying to catch his breath. "They're Prefects!"

"Got a better idea?" Eddington raised one eyebrow, his eyes determined.

The footsteps came up the stairs again, getting closer and closer to their room.

"Stay in the bathroom!"

The footsteps grew louder. Eddington retreated into the room and crouched alongside the bed. Tom was well hidden in the bathroom, waiting for the Prefects to come.

"Here's an open door," one of the Prefects said.

"Strange. Did you hear that earlier?"

"What?"

"Some coughing sounds coming from this room."

"You think there might be someone there?"

"No. Proceed."

Eddington tightened his grip on the rod. His heart was racing as the shoes of the Prefects creaked the carpeted floor.

"What the—"

Eddington heard the spray go off.

"Christ—"

"Ed! Where are you?"

A deep breath. Eddington rushed up to the Prefects and gave the dark-suited bores two good thwacks on their heads. For a second, she was back. He saw her again. He could feel the warmth of her hand as she whispered: *Walk with me...*

But then there was The Regime, and it was all there was. Everything looked black and white without her. Where could she be? Amelia? For a split second, Archer's face appeared. Eddington clenched his teeth and gripped the rod tighter, then gave another two blows.

Hate.

The two dark suits fell to the ground together with their empty crates. Eddington clenched the rod and gave their heads a few more blows until he could see the red oozing out, coloring the end of his weapon.

"Ed!"

Face splattered with speckles of blood, Eddington let out a long, deep breath and collapsed to the ground. A broad smile consumed his face.

"Ed! Oh, God!" Tom wore circles in the carpet as he paced around the room. "This is... we're dead. We're so—"

Eddington moved himself a bit closer to the corpses and tugged at their black blazers. "You've got a better idea?"

The blood continued to stain the carpeted floor, but none of it went on the dark suits. Tom and Eddington were dressed in black; their own clothing covered the two corpses on the ground. They passed by the bathroom mirrors and straightened their ties.

"You sure we won't get..."

"Just play it well." Eddington straightened the lapels of Tom's coat. "Looking good."

"Ed, I'm—"

"Don't be. Hold this." Eddington raised one of the crates into Tom's palms and smiled.

Tom gripped the crate, and Eddington picked up the other. Their footsteps echoed down the hallway, and they descended the stairs.

Chapter 26

"All clear?" the guardsman of the truck asked. His voice was muffled by his riot mask.

"Yes." Eddington kept a straight face, trying to ignore the gun and baton attached to the guard's belt despite his wariness of them.

"Okay." The guardsman got into the truck and, right before he closed the door, said, "Hold on, we're going."

Eddington nodded. The two crates were placed at the back of the truck along with the other books. Tom and Eddington looked at one another and gripped the side rails of the truck, then they took off.

The truck was fast, but the road was smooth. All the places Eddington knew so well—the café, the orderly streets, those back alleyways—passed by in a blur as they glided through the streets. No tinge of sadness or nostalgia overwhelmed him. Instead, relief flooded his body. Everything that had happened no longer mattered. He was free. The Regime still lived on, but he was escaping beyond The Wall. L'Académie was fading away from his mind. He was going to see the world for the first time.

The truck rolled to a stop at the gates of The Wall. Guards still lined up along the border, grasping machine guns as they stood motionless. The driver waved to the sentry, and the gray concrete door rolled open, allowing the truck to pass through. Overhead, two signal indicators on top of the door beeped and flashed as the vehicle slowly passed by the guards' scanning sights.

Beyond the door, the last relics of civilization outside of the Regime rotted in the distance, standing like forgotten memorials to a dying god. Decayed gas stations and crumbling buildings were making their final stand as nature slowly erased them. Long cracks ran through the road the truck traveled on. Eddington looked back at where the gate to The Regime was, but he could no longer see it. They were beyond The Wall, and that was all there was.

Soon the truck passed by what used to be another city. On the horizon, Eddington saw the frames of a fallen bridge rusting away. Weeds sprouted like wildfire on what used to be a riverbed, slowly eating away the scattered pieces of concrete and steel. Branches extended every which way, shooting off and hovering over the path. The road wound between half-fallen buildings, and the driver slowed to carefully avoid shards of glass on the road. Occasionally Eddington saw spray-painted signs on the sides of remaining buildings. A few miles down, he even saw burning barrels. Some stragglers still survived among the cracks. They were well hidden, but they were there. It was hard to imagine what kind of life they led in such rotten corners.

Beyond The Wall, he found a world of lawless chaos. It held nothing but man's rotting creations under an indifferent sky. He couldn't even imagine any books survived there. At least The Regime had books. Eddington took a deep breath and tried to find answers in the gray clouds, but there were none. He looked toward Tom, who stared at the streets, motionless.

Another burning barrel passed their view, but that time Eddington saw someone. He only noted her tattered clothing; the truck barreled by too quickly to notice details. His stomach dropped.

Rogues.

He tried to bring back to mind the little forest and the trickling stream, but it was impossible against the grim backdrop. He kept asking himself what had happened to the world, but there were no answers. It was prohibited.

The truck took a few more turns and eventually progressed past the deserted, nameless city. The sky started to clear, but the scenery didn't brighten. The road was the only mark of order; all else was left to nature. Eddington saw deserted barns in the distance, slowly crumpling into the ground. Small houses along the way were missing windows and rooftops. The Regime was the only law holding back nature, the only place where things were running.

A gray speck in the distance disrupted the muted colors of chaos. It became larger and larger, and Eddington recognized it as another Wall. The black dots floating around it were probably guards. The truck stopped. The driver waved at the sentinel, and the blast door opened as the truck entered another district.

Tom was a stranger to the new district, but not Eddington. Immediately he sensed something from the streets. Though there were changes, Eddington still remembered. He used to roam around that place. There was the baker, the post, the bookshop—well, the *closed* bookshop. People who roamed the streets didn't have colored blazers, but they were all dressed in identical raincoats over formal suits. The Regime had changed the details, but what was in Eddington's head, hidden amongst those dreams, came back and anchored themselves in the streets. The truck passed by a storefront that looked like The Corner from District-E, but for some reason, Eddington jolted when he saw it. That used to be where his house was. Right around the corner was where his father was arrested.

The truck made a turn off-road. Green invaded the scene. Trees, once scarce along the passing streets, appeared. The gray pavements were replaced by patches of grass along the off-road trail. The truck eventually stopped at another checkpoint with guardsmen. A sign announced "Conservation" at the front. The guardsmen nodded as the wire fence scraped open.

As the truck drove through the forest, Eddington turned his head and saw a stream. Most of it flowed, but small slivers of ice stayed on top of it. The current tapped gently against the rocks below, trickling, trickling—Amelia in her white sleeveless dress, whispering, whispering.

***

The truck jolted to a stop. Tom quickly composed himself as Eddington looked at the driver.

275

"We're here." The guardsman next to the driver got out of the truck, still uptight and proper. Eddington and Tom hopped off the side railing and attempted to tame their mussed hair.

"Standard protocol," the guardsman said, leaning against a stack of books on the back of the truck.

"No problem, sir." Eddington nodded.

"Snap it back, aback. Left, right, swift, in, out."

"Got it." Eddington nodded again, unsure of what to do next. He picked up a crate and filled it with books from the back. Tom followed suit.

They walked along a paved concrete track. The gray capsule became visible between the trees as they walked toward it. There were two other guardsmen standing watch in front.

"All done?" The one on the left lowered his gun.

"Yes."

"Ready?" The one on the right said as they both turned to the capsule.

"Yes."

"One, two, three."

The two guards turned keys at the same time. The blast door of the capsule opened as a gush of wind rushed out.

"Again, bottom well, shelves, in, out, done. No access to the other levels."

"Yes," Eddington said.

The two went into the capsule, and the blast wall closed up. They were on a platform that descended slowly downward.

"Ed—"

"Not now." Eddington didn't turn his head.

"What are we supposed to—"

"Shut up…"

"There are hundreds of feet between them and us." Tom was trying to hide his fear, but his voice trembled.

"They might still hear us." Eddington's eyes were fixed on the door.

"But we're technically—"

"No. Careful."

Eddington and Tom jolted as the platform clanked to a stop. The blast door grated open again, but the two of them stood frozen. They were speechless.

The room curved around in a circle, and shelves upon shelves of books stretched above them. Eddington craned his neck to see the ceiling, but the space was so vast, it seemed endless. Each book had its own compartment with green indicators below them. Two shelves near Eddington and Tom were not yet filled. Instead of green, the indicators below those compartments blinked orange. Occasionally, slivers of light ran through the gaps between the compartments and made a whirring noise. After the initial shock, the two stepped out of the elevator.

"I think we leave them... Tom?"

Tom's eyes were glued to the shelves surrounding him. "*This* is where all that—" he mumbled.

"I know. But we must hurry." Eddington walked up to one of the shelves and left the crate at the foot of it.

"Al-all right." Tom slowly took a few more steps away from the elevator's shaft with his crate in his hand. "This is—"

"Come on, Tom! Hurry."

Tom's shoes tapped against the floor, which made an echo in the sterile space. He still couldn't tear his eyes away from the shelves of the books. He set down his crate next to Eddington.

"Okay, now. Quick, there are more crates out there." Eddington walked toward the elevator, but Tom stayed put.

"Ed?" Tom's eyes were empty. He curled his lips and narrowed his eyes to what looked like a smile against his will. Then he retraced his eyes from one shelf to the next before taking one step at a time to a shelf. "Ed, this is beautiful."

Eddington stared at Tom, wide-eyed.

You think people from L'Académie could handle this?

"Ed?" Tom stopped at the foot of a shelf and turned around, tears streaming down his eyes. "All of them... all of them, Ed. They're here."

"Tom." Eddington took a few steps toward Tom while glancing up at the security cameras on the ceiling. "Don't be stupid."

"On our way here, Ed"—Tom continued to cry and smile—"I saw the city. I saw what it's like beyond The Wall. It was beautiful." He wiped his tears. "Two more months, and I'd be out, Ed. Out into that? Out to... out to *that*?" He collapsed on his knees. "Ha! L'Académie. Ha! Ha ha!"

"Tom?" Eddington rushed up to him.

"Ed!" Tom stood up, still with that smile. "No. You know what? Look here." Tom walked up to one of the shelves and ripped a few books out of their compartments. The room darkened as the indicators below those compartments turned red. An alarm came on as the blast door of the elevator closed. "What've we got here?" He opened a few of those books.

"Tom!"

He went up to another shelf and pulled out a few more books. The lights in the room were blinking.

"You need to stop this now!" Eddington gripped Tom's shoulders.

"Whoa! Whoa!" Tom said as he back away from him. "Easy. Looked here!" He cracked open another book, thumbing along the line. "I am conscious of my own existence as determined in time," he recited.

"Tom!" The floor turned dark as the alarm kept going.

"And here: I was standing in front of her, stunned, disgraced, hideously embarrassed, and, I think, smiling." Those lights blinked and blinked. In the brief intervals of light, Eddington saw a silhouette next to one of the shelves.

"All around me! There was still the luminous, sun-drenched countryside. The glare! From the sky! Was unbearable! Unbearable!"

Eddington tried to follow the silhouette, but the figure disappeared in the darkness. "What in the…" He turned to look at Tom. "He's…" Immediately, he ran up to him and grabbed him again. "Tom, too much, you've taken in way too much!"

"Shut up!" Tom began to sob and pushed Eddington away. He went up to another shelf and pulled out a few more books. Red indicators kept on blinking. He flipped through an array of books, a wild look taking root in his eyes. "A knavish speech sleeps in a foolish ear! O! Brave new world that has such people in it! To a nunnery, go! Farewell!"

Eddington tried restraining him, but Tom gave him a forceful blow, and he fell over onto a pile of scattered books with a dizzy head. Another flash of light amidst the chaos, the silhouette passed his eyes again. The figure had a long coat and long hair. The lights darkened again, and Eddington struggled up from a pile of scattered books.

"Pure orthodoxy! Party member. All but unthinking minds!"

Eddington ran up to Tom and tackled him to the floor.

"It was a pleasure to burn!" There was a grin on his face.

"You've got to stop this! Stop!" Eddington tried to keep him at bay.

"The world is all that there is! Send me to an Island? Iceland? Land? Hark!" Tom headbutted Eddington in the nose, and with a crisp snap, a sharp pain coursed through his skull and watered his eyes. He collapsed to the ground as Tom loomed over him. Tom knelt down; his eyes told the story of some sort of desperate madness, and his hand wrapped around Eddington's neck. He squeezed harder; Eddington pried at his hands, seeking relief, but they were too strong. "Ed. I didn't want to do this. We're beyond The Wall! You get it? Beyond The Wall! We're free!" The grip tightened.

Eddington's vision blurred. The alarm still blinked the lights in The Archive, and in another interval of light, Tom laughed as his grip remained tight.

Another interval of light. The figure moved close to the two, and it seemed to be holding something in its hand. "Stop."

Eddington froze. Before he had the chance to remember who it was, blood splattered across his face.

"Tom!"

The body fell limply toward the stacks he scattered. The red blood dyed the pages. The alarm was still on, but all the lights were restored. Eddington turned his head and was blinded for a moment by bright lights; all he could do was stammer at the figure holding the gun.

Chapter 27

Eddington stayed still on the floor next to Tom's body while Archer pointed the gun at him. The alarm of The Archive ceased, and the blast door opened. "Took you a while." Archer walked up to Eddington. Two Prefects guarded the blast door behind them.

"You…" Eddington wiped the blood from his broken nose and tried to get up onto his feet.

"Ah, ah, ah." Archer taunted with his gun. "Don't be ridiculous."

"You…" Eddington clenched both of his fists when kneeling on the ground.

"You still have questions." Archer crept toward Eddington. "Okay. Now, this is it." The lights in The Archive flickered into a clinical white. Everyone was wearing black.

"Get to the fucking point!" Eddington's yell echoed in The Archive's chamber. "What are you? *Where is she*?"

Archer chuckled and knelt down next to Eddington and patted him on the shoulder, "Why don't you just look." He reached into his pocket and pulled out the picture of Amelia. "There she is. Isn't she the only reason you're here? How're your memories coming along?" Archer smiled again. "You two were so close. Just inseparable. I told you I liked this forest too."

"You… you…" Eddington looked at a face with a familiar smile on the photo.

Walk with me.

Archer closed his eyes and stood back up. "It's about time I break it to you." He lowered his gun and looked at the two Prefects behind him. "There's no getting out of The Regime. Did you see what was beyond The Wall?"

Eddington stared at Archer without a word.

"It's a wasteland out there. We had to organize the last of our resources into little districts." Archer took a deep breath. "Stability, Ed. We can't afford to lose this place. All of us went through the same thing. We're the only ones who're able to experience what they call The Cross without losing it." Archer said. "Prefects are great for enforcing hard rules." He turned to look at the Prefects. "But us, we're here to make sure knowledge doesn't become a disease. We're the viruses of the system."

Eddington looked at Tom's limp corpse.

"Three in a row." Archer followed Eddington's gaze. "That's what happens if citizens come in contact with knowledge not meant for them. We have to be free-thinking agents if we want to lure out these threats. The disease."

"But this isn't... isn't..." Eddington muttered while looking at Archer. "This isn't an education..."

"It's what we have, and it works," Archer said. "And you're going to help us to keep what's left of it."

"This isn't a..." Eddington shifted his eyes to the photo.

"Oh, her." Archer raised his eyebrows. "I thought you'd surely remember her."

Eddington stayed still, and tears rolled down from his eyes.

"Did you remember what happened?"

***

The young man walked past many former lecture rooms. The rooms were stripped of desks, lecterns, and projector screens. The walls were painted white; beds replaced comfortable couches and desks meant for studying. In the once-busy corridors, the people passing to and fro with lively conversations were gone; in their place were hushed sounds and living ghosts.

He turned into the room. A window overlooked the front courtyard, and the girl lay in bed. He cleared his throat, but she didn't open her eyes.

The young man stood in front of the window and took a deep breath. She was there; his heart was settled, but her sickness worried him. The young man's breath fogged the glass. It wasn't snowing, but the cool breezes outside shook the branches and brushed against the blades of grass.

He held a book in his hands. He turned around and sat on the edge of the bed, pressing his hand gently against hers. Slowly, she opened her eyes, though they were only open a crack. She jerked a little in her weak frame and smiled as her eyes began to water. He sat there as sour churns swelled up in his chest, traveling into his nose, obscuring his vision.

"You promised to read something to me." The smiling cheeks were accompanied by traces of tears.

"Yes." The young man sobbed, but her smile overpowered the sorrowed heart.

"It's fine." She smiled again. "You're still that little worm from the bookshop." She reached out but was too weak to bring herself to him. The young man leaned toward her, allowing her hand to ruffle his dark-brown hair.

"You'll get better."

"Hopefully." Another smile. More tears rolled down her cheeks.

"Amelia." Eddington squeezed her hand. "I... I..."

"Spit it out." She slowly raised the back of her left sleeve to wipe the tears.

"I—"

***

Eddington looked at Archer with wide eyes.

"I hated to see her go too," Archer said. "I felt the same. I saw you two grow up together, and that horrible disease took her from us." He shook his head. "But then I made another mistake. I thought maybe if I put you through L'Académie, you'd forget about all of the mess, but I was wrong."

A sliver of silence.

"So, you've all your memories now?" Archer stood back up. "You think you've read enough? Seen enough?"

"So... you're saying... you're saying Amelia wasn't..."

"You fool. She wasn't captured. She died before I ordered them to send you to Académie. I wanted what was good for you, but sometimes..." Archer looked around him at all the books. "L'Académie is powerful, but it can't change our nature, Ed."

"Then why did they…" Eddington pressed himself up from the ground. "Why did they arrest you near the tree?"

"It was protocol. A training program, if you will, and you're the next in line." He pulled out a cigarette and lighted it. "Because before I know it, I'll be gone too. This horrible disease."

Chapter 28

The blast door opened, and Eddington and Archer stepped out. Sunrays beamed through the clouds into the woven branches, casting spotted shadows on the concrete platform of The Archive's entrance. Archer ordered the two Prefects to stay put, placed a hand on Eddington's shoulder, and signaled him to follow. Together, they went off into the woods and followed the sound of the stream, eventually ending up at the tree stump.

"I kept this place around just for you," he said. "I'll give you a minute."

Eddington didn't say anything and walked toward the stump. The blades of grass dampened his shoes, and he sat down on it over the trickling stream. Archer stood behind him and smoked. The mirage rose above the trees into the sky and loomed over The Regime.

Eddington sat up a little straighter and heard the bird chirp. It startled him a little because those sounds existed only in his dreams. He looked down and realized he was holding a book and was no longer wearing a Prefect's suit. The clouds parted, and the scene brightened, and he felt those arms around his skinny frame again.

"Hi."

He turned around and saw the girl in the white dress whispering into his ear.

"You promised."

Eddington smiled and opened up his book. "Yes, I did. Yes, I did…" Tears streamed down his cheeks onto the pages and smudged the ink.

"This is where you belong, Ed. Isn't it pretty here? A little paradise? Our little secret spot?" The girl giggled. "Let's stay here together forever. Promise me you'll stay with me forever." She stretched out her hand. "Walk with me."

Eddington looked at her and tucked his book under his arm.

Walk with me.

He stood up and turned away from the tree stump.

Let's stay here forever.

He walked along the stream leading to The Archive, still with that smile about his face. The Prefects watched his moves while Archer smoked his cigarette in his long dark coat and kept still.

Eddington knelt down, dipped his fingers into the cold stream, and shook his head. Little sobs came through the woods and soon turned into a howl. He started splashing the water and soaked his head in the stream. Archer stood by and extinguished his cigarette in the soil. By then, Eddington was entirely in the stream, howling and splashing.

"That's it." Archer waved at the two Prefects.

Take him away.

***

Back in District-E, things were still running in a clockwork familiar to the citizens. Students were separated into different factions by different colors. The Box still carried loads of students off at The Square. L'Académie still educated a useful workforce. Prefects stalked the streets with their backs erect and expressions blank, and once in a while, a figure in a long coat drifted from one alley to the next, always on the move and always on the lookout.

- The End -

About the Author

R. C. Waldun is a writer, speaker, and social critic based in Melbourne, Australia whose work mainly consists of criticisms of the modern education system and ways toward a better literary education. For more information and creative projects, head to rcwaldun.com.

Printed in Great Britain
by Amazon